Don Juaneen

John Broderick was born in Athlone in 1927. Educated in Ireland, he has lived in London, Rome and Paris. Although his novels have been the cause of much controversy in his native country, he was elected a member of the Irish Academy of Letters in 1968. His other novels include *The Fugitives*, *The Pilgrimage*, *The Waking of Willie Ryan*, *An Apology for Roses* and *A Pride of Summer*.

He is also a regular contributor to various Irish newspapers and magazines and broadcasts on the radio.

Previously published by
John Broderick in Pan Books

John Broderick

Don Juaneen

Pan Books London and Sydney

First published 1963 by Weidenfeld and Nicolson Ltd
This edition published 1978 by Pan Books Ltd,
Cavaye Place, London SW10 9PG
2nd printing 1979
© John Broderick 1963
ISBN 0 330 25415 4
Printed and bound in Great Britain by
Hunt Barnard Printing Ltd, Aylesbury, Bucks.

1

AFTER twenty-five years Mr Quill still had to read the instructions before making a call in a public telephone booth. Should one put in the pennies before or after lifting the receiver? And was it three or fourpence now? It used to be two when Mr Quill first came to Dublin. He could remember that very well. He paused, his small white hand resting on the coin-box, and fell into a reverie.

He was eighteen; and he had exactly two pennies left in his pocket as he got off the train and followed the red-haired girl out of Westland Row station; down the long stone steps, dragging his cardboard case beside him like a reluctant and overfed dog; on to the path in time to see her go into the telephone booth at the other side of the street. And then the traffic lumbered by, cutting them off for a full two minutes. Time for her to make her call, step out of the booth, stop a taxi which appeared like magic when she raised her green eyes to look for one, and drive off leaving a spatter of mud on the trousers of Mr Quill's best, and only, blue suit. He could think of nothing else to do except step into the booth after her. The stuffy little glass box was filled with the synthetic scent of lilacs, the scent which had filled the railway carriage during the two-and-a-half hours he had shared it with the red-haired girl and the elderly parish priest with whom she had carried on an easy and animated conversation, which did not for one moment include Mr Quill. It was a cheap scent; but Mr Quill did not know this. He lingered for ten minutes in the booth, savouring the romance of it, and pretending to read the instructions. His twopence was safe: he knew no one in Dublin.

Now, he put on his spectacles, read the instructions again, lifted the receiver and dropped three pennies into the box. He dialled his number, which he had used many times in the last few years, but could not remember either, and kept written down on an old envelope in his wallet. As he heard the sinister little sound of the bell ringing at the connecting end, he experienced the familiar confusion of panic which always descended on him whenever he rang Philip O'Connor; a panic which once or twice forced him to put down the receiver before he got a reply. But today he knew he had to go through with it. He had his speech prepared. First of all the maid would answer—

'Hullo. Could I speak to Mr O'Connor, please?'

'Speaking.'

Mr Quill was knocked off his course. This was the first time that Philip had ever answered the telephone himself.

'Oh,' said Mr Quill helplessly. 'Oh.'

'Who's speaking?' Philip's voice was cool, remote, terrifying.

'Is that you, Philip?'

'Yes, John.' Philip was always good on the telephone, calm and self-possessed as he was in everything. Mr Quill cleared his throat and began again.

'How did you know it was me?' His spectacles grew clouded in the steamy atmosphere of the booth, and he made an effort to take them off.

'How are you?' said Philip.

'Oh, I'm great, great. How are you?' Mr Quill tried to push his spectacles into his breast pocket with his free hand, but they caught in the wire and slipped from his damp fingers on to the floor. He looked down at them and blinked.

'Where are you?'

'I'm, ah, I'm ringing from the office.' Mr Quill's short-sighted eyes glanced restlessly about the glass coffin: he felt trapped.

'Working late.' There was a note of amusement in Philip's voice.

'That's right. Listen Philip could I see you this evening ?'

'I'm afraid not, John. Lilian and I are going out this evening. It's a bit of a bore, but we can't get out of it. Would Wednesday suit you ?'

'Oh, yes, Philip, that would suit me fine. I just thought —'

'About eight,' said Philip in a tone that did not call for an answer. 'How's Sybil ?'

'Oh, she's great, great. She was asking for you.'

'Well, goodbye John. I'll see you on Wednesday.' The line clicked dead. Mr Quill held the receiver to his ear for a few moments. When Philip's business was finished he said goodbye and put down the phone. Mr Quill had never been able to do this: he went on muttering about the weather, about anything that came into his head, until his mind went blank, or the other person cut him off. He had never learned how to dismiss anybody.

He picked up his spectacles from the floor and pushed the door open with his shoulder. Two people waiting outside gave him the usual dirty look as he stepped out on to the path. Mr Quill did not see them: he was looking up at the huge granite façade of the Government Department where he had worked all his adult life, along with a couple of thousand other officials, all of whom he had allowed to leave the building before him so that he could make his call in private. On either side of the monolithic structure the shabby Georgian houses were plum-red in the afternoon sunlight. Mr Quill felt its rays warming his back as he turned and walked up the street: slowly, for he was a big man and a little overweight; precisely, not without a self-conscious sense of balance, for his feet were small; apparently aimlessly, for his hands were clasped behind his back. His blue suit fitted him a little tightly about the hips; but it was neat and well-pressed; and his white Sunday shirt was reasonably untarnished at the end of an uneventful Monday.

He was wondering whether he ought to go into the pub around the corner where some of his colleagues would at half past five on a fine June afternoon be finishing off their pints and making a bolt for home. Mr Quill decided against it. He had been restless and nervous all day thinking of his telephone call; and his colleagues in the office, drinking tea, reading the racing papers, gossiping, and handling official documents as if they were anonymous letters, had got on his nerves. He would work his way home, and stop at Mick's Lounge where, at this hour, he would be sure of meeting Paul.

He turned the corner into the lane where he parked his car; got in, put on his spectacles, and drove off, gripping the wheel anxiously as he turned into Stephen's Green because he had never got used to the city traffic. And then, right outside the Shelbourne Hotel in the middle of the rush-hour confusion, the ancient Ford spluttered, gurgled, and stopped dead, with its tarnished bonnet pointing east.

2

NEVERTHELESS Mr Quill got there. With the help of a sympathetic Guard who came from Mr Quill's home-town the car was pushed into a side-lane, locked; and its owner boarded a bus. Twenty-five minutes later he descended carefully—since he did not use his spectacles in public except when he was reading or driving—at a stop a hundred yards from Mick's Lounge where there was another telephone booth. This time there was no need for him to look up the number; nor had he any feeling of panic: he was only ringing his wife.

'Hullo, hullo, is that you Sybil? This is me.'

'Where are you? Is anything wrong?' His wife's voice lost the sharp refined note she used when answering the telephone, and became flat.

'I'm in Stephen's Green. I was just turning the car home when it stopped dead outside the Shelbourne. I had an awful time trying to get it pushed into the side. I don't know—'

'Will you be home for your tea because I'm cooking a chop for you?'

'Listen Sybil I can't leave the car like this. I'll have to try and get somebody to fix it.'

'What am I going to do with the chop?'

'Well Caroline can eat it can't she?'

'She's not coming home. She has a tennis-club meeting tonight, and she's having tea with the Richardsons. I told you that at breakfast.'

'Well, why can't you eat the chop yourself, Sybil? Is it a nice chop?'

'I have another one down for myself. You don't expect me to eat the two do you?'

'Well leave it in the oven. I'll take it when I get home.'

'What time will you be home?'

'I don't know. I have to wait for this mechanic—'

'If you didn't insist on driving that old crock. Why can't we have a new car like everybody else? Anyway I have to go out.'

'Out where?'

'I told you that at breakfast too. I have to go and visit old Miss Blake.'

'Well, I'll be home as soon as I can.'

'Oh, all right.'

Mr Quill stepped out of the booth, and walked slowly down the path towards Mick's. Intersecting streets led on his left down to the sea; a sea which in Mr Quill's short-sighted eyes blended with the sky, where the blunt-nosed promontory of Howth Head floated like some enormous, anachronistic dirigible. On such a fine evening all the sailing boats were out. He stopped and watched. Although he lived only a mile farther along the coast at Sandycove, he had never outlived his delight at the sight of the sleek sails gliding out of Dun Laoghaire harbour, and floating into the sky at Dublin Bay like low-flying seagulls. He had once put on his spectacles to watch them; but the sharp clear outlines had disappointed him. They were far more beautiful in the gentle haze of his normal vision. Mr Quill stood watching them with a smile on his full lips for a few minutes; then, his hands clasped behind his back, he walked on towards the pub. The evening stretched before him, free, empty and sunny.

Mick's was one of those old Dublin public houses which have been turned into lounges by putting in a terrazzo front of mottled green, a terrazzo floor of mottled pink, painting the four walls in different colours, lemon, orange, red, and blue, and placing three leather-topped stools in front of the bar-counter. But it smelled as it had always done: of stout; sawdust, which the proprietor still threw on the floor behind the counter for old times' sake; and alcoholic urine from the lavatory, newly tiled and whitewashed, but still strategically placed inside the front door. All this Mr Quill, who was conservative, and whose sense of smell was extremely keen, felt very comforting.

His entrance was impressive. He came in with that casual air of preoccupation which sometimes accompanies self-confidence, but which in his case was due to myopia. He could not see the expressions on the dim faces pointed towards the door. Not that any of them, all connoisseurs of the physical defect, the misplaced step, the exaggerated mannerism, could deny that he was a handsome man with his great height, his broad shoulders, his clear blue eyes, ruddy cheeks and thick curling hair. The worst any of them could say about him was that he looked like a policeman in civvies. And this was exactly what Paul Shine was thinking at that moment.

He was sitting in his usual place just inside the door facing the lavatory, away from the other habitués who tended to cluster together near the stove—now out for the summer—at the back of the pub. As usual, he was reading a book, smoking a cigarette, drinking whiskey, and wearing the same black suit he had had on when Mr Quill first made his acquaintance ten years ago.

'Why,' he said, closing his book and sitting on it, 'don't you wear a hat? If you did you might pass for an inspector or even a superintendent of the police. As it is you look like a Guard, a Guard who has missed promotion.'

Mr Quill raised his finger to the proprietor for the usual, and sat down opposite Paul. He ran his fingers through his thick black hair, and grinned.

'I will when I begin to go grey,' he said. Mr Quill was proud of his black curls which he imagined took ten years off his age.

'Not even if you go egg-bald,' remarked Paul, dipping his finger in the whiskey and applying it to a pimple he had on the tip of his long pointed nose. 'People who don't grow up never wear hats. I've often noticed it.'

'Poor Paul,' laughed his friend happily as his pint arrived, and he lit the first cigarette of the evening. He stretched himself lazily and sighed hugely. Paul winced.

'There's no need to blow me off the chair.'

'*Slainte!*' Mr Quill raised his glass.

'You're late this evening. What happened? Did the old crock break down again?'

Mr Quill's heavy eyelids drooped, and he looked at Paul through his thick black lashes. The corners of his mouth curled in a little secret smile.

'No, Paul, the old crock did not break down. It never does except when I want it to for reasons of my own. All I'm sorry for is that I'm not a bit later.'

Paul raised himself six inches from his chair and took out his book, which he turned round and then sat down on it again.

'I don't know how it is but one side of a book always seems to be more comfortable than the other.' He settled himself and applied another dab of whiskey to his pimple.

'All the same,' went on Mr Quill dreamily, 'it wasn't time wasted. Not that anything happened this afternoon, but it's coming on, it certainly is. She had to rush home today because they have visitors, but she's going to have lunch with me tomorrow.'

'Why don't you just go out and pick up a tart? God knows there are enough of them hanging around in Dublin. Not that they get much change out of the men in this country. It's a good thing the tourist season is starting. I pity the poor things. The tarts, I mean.'

'I wouldn't have anything to do with prostitutes,' retorted Mr Quill with feeling. 'A disgusting lot, and most of them foreigners. No decent Irish girl would carry on like that.'

Paul snorted and fingered his nose tenderly.

'No,' went on Mr Quill, 'I like them with a bit of class. Now take this girl I'm talking about. Such skin and hair and ankles and hands. And the way she dresses!' He raised his hand with the thumb and forefinger joined, a gesture he always made when he was describing something really special.

'I know all about her skin. You told me about it before. What's her name anyhow?'

Mr Quill frowned into his pint. He wiped the froth fastidiously from his lips before he replied.

'You don't really expect me to tell you that, do you? I'm not a man that goes about boasting over women behind their backs. I have more respect for them.'

Paul finished his glass and poured out another from the bottle he bought every evening.

'Like hell you have. What were you doing making a telephone call down the street before you came in here? I went out next door to get the paper, and I saw you coming out. Why couldn't you make it here?'

Mr Quill shifted uneasily in his chair; but only for a moment. Then he closed his eyes and scratched his chest lazily.

'It was a call of a private nature. I couldn't make it here with the whole pub listening. Besides, she'd know well from the hum in the background that I was talking from a pub.'

'Jesus, what kind of a girl is she?'

Mr Quill remained silent, savouring the moment.

'It takes you a quarter of an hour to get out here, well maybe twenty minutes in that old crock, and the minute you get here you start ringing her up. A girl that doesn't approve of pubs. What kind of a fool are you?' Paul took out his book, patted it fussily, and sat down on it again.

'It wasn't the girl I was ringing,' said Mr Quill quietly. 'It was my wife.'

Mr Quill was an artist. Never too much of a good thing; nothing crude; a supple feeling for probability that was more convincing than the truth. The physical sense of balance which carried his big body so truly upon its little feet; his neat and sober clothes; the restraint, the exact timing of his gestures, were all reflected in his mind. It was only when he was telling the truth that Mr Quill was clumsy.

'Oh,' said Paul, taken aback. 'Oh, Sybil.' Paul understood from his friend that Sybil Quill disapproved entirely of drinking; and that his evenings in Mick's were the result of a victory in a long fight for freedom.

'Of course I have her broken in now. You have to show a woman who's the boss. At the same time you have to make certain concessions. We don't talk about Mick's, although she knows well I come here whenever I feel like it. I was firm on that. But there's no point in sticking your neck out, especially with the other thing in the background.'

Paul nodded. He was convinced by the bit about the concessions. He did not like things to be too simple.

'Well, now,' said Mr Quill genially, secure in his position as an expert in feminine psychology, 'how's business?'

Paul sighed, and took a long drink of whiskey.

'Rotten. It's the summer, and everybody is saving up for the holidays. Mother of Victories is still all right, the prize money is so big they can't resist it, and the Tomb of the Apostles is fair. But Blessed Mary Magda O'Hara is gone to hell. I told them that a pilgrimage to Lourdes is no draw for anybody now. Everybody's been there. What they want is hard cash. Nobody will take a card out if the money is less than five hundred, and the competition is awful. It was all right until the Jesuits started, but you know what they are. They're offering a thousand.' He lowered his voice, and glanced uneasily round the pub. 'And they're cutting the prices too, I know it for a fact.'

Paul made his living by selling shares in the innumerable raffles, sweeps, draws, and gambling games which were run in the city for charitable purposes by the various religious Orders. As a promoter he was entitled to a prize if one of his clients won. As he had more than three hundred cards, each with ten or more names on it, there were few weeks when he did not make ten or twenty pounds. Paul drank only twelve-year-old whiskey; and he had a fine taste in wines. But he ate only sandwiches.

'Put me down for three shares in the Tomb of the Apostles,' said Mr Quill.

'Three shillings, please.'

3

SHE waited in the shadow of the church porch, a tall, somewhat angular girl, a little uneasily dressed in a light summer frock. She ran her fingers along the rim of the low-cut bodice, and adjusted the black lace mantilla which she had thrown over her head before entering the church.

Her hands were small with long tapering fingers, a little stained by cigarette smoke. She wore no make-up; but her colouring was good, and the fine bones under her brown healthy skin gave her a certain aristocratic air, which her manner, somewhat remote and preoccupied, emphasized. She stood, a little apart from the people who passed in and out about her, in a small pool of silence: an aura which she was not as yet aware was quite natural to her. She was eighteen years of age.

The big, panther-like Mercedes, its glistening black flanks powdered with the dust of the summer roads, drew up at the end of the path on the opposite side to the church. She tore the mantilla from her head and ran down the steps, hurrying across the gravel with the slightly duck-like carriage of the tall woman who wears flat-heeled shoes to conceal her height.

The man sitting behind the wheel of the Mercedes did not look around as she approached. There was something lizard-like in the immobility of his small neat profile with its regular features framed by the open window of the car. He was smoking a cigarette, his hand resting on the driving-wheel. When the girl crossed the road behind the car he started the engine and reached out to open the door. She slipped into the seat beside him, and the big car glided off.

She put her hand into his pocket and took out a packet of cigarettes. He pressed a lighter in the dashboard, and she bent down swiftly and kissed his hand before lighting her cigarette.

'Don't do that,' he said sharply, snatching his hand away.

The girl put the cigarettes back into his jacket pocket, and kept her hand there. Very gently he disengaged himself, holding her wrist between his thumb and fore-finger, and placing her hand back on her lap.

'Where are we going?' she said, leaning forward and touching the glass of the window with her forehead.

'I don't know. Some place.'

She laughed, throwing herself back against her seat with the exaggerated abandon of the very young. The man looked at her briefly, a curious expression, half sly, half amused, flickering across his pale face.

'Don't you care?' he said in his cold clipped voice, a curious voice, at once light and deep.

She shook her head, and touched his arm with her fingertips. This time he made no effort to disengage himself; but he leaned forward, gripping the wheel as the car began to climb the narrow winding road above Killiney Bay. As they came on to the flat stretch of road overlooking the dazzling crescent of water she held her hands up before her face, framing the view.

'Oh, Philip, this is the first time we've been here since we met.'

'The Sunday promenade on Vico Road,' he said with a little chuckle. 'How bored you looked.'

'I was. Two months next Sunday. It seems like another world.'

'How long have you?' he asked, sliding into a lower gear as they climbed the little hump in front of the gates of Victoria Hill.

'I told them I had a tennis-club meeting. That often goes on until ten.'

'And they believed you?'

'Of course.'

They began to descend the steep hill beyond the village, and the view of the great bay disappeared behind high stone garden walls. Half-way down the incline he turned up a narrow lane and pulled up outside a huge pair of iron gates, with a little red lodge inside on the left, half-hidden behind a mass of laurels.

'Where are we going?' she asked.

The man got out and opened the gates with a big key he took out of his pocket. He got back into the car and they drove through.

'The lodge is empty,' he said. 'They use it for garden tools.'

'Aren't you going to close the gates?'

'It isn't necessary. Nobody comes here.'

They drove slowly along the short avenue, skirted a wide lawn, and drew up in front of a big Victorian villa with yellow stucco walls covered with Virginia creeper. The trees rustled like taffeta when the engine was switched off, and birds fluttered away from the eaves.

'Who lives here?' she demanded, sitting up very straight and peering at the glass door that led on to a flagged terrace in front of the house, overlooking the lawn.

'Friends of mine. They're away at present. I have the key.'

'They trust you with it?' she said with awkward playfulness; relieved now that she knew she had nobody to meet.

'Of course. I'm the sort of man people trust—with houses.'

She got out of the car and walked over to the edge of the lawn.

'Oh,' she cried, 'Philip, look.'

He looked at her with a slight smile, but did not follow her pointing finger across the lawn and the banked hydrangeas to where the sea and the smoky mountains and the oily green valley of Shanganagh spread out before her: the view that she had cupped together a few minutes before. It was like stained glass through which a brilliant light filtered; segments of blue and green and silver-white; flickering under the milky sun; glowing and formal; but seen here from a different angle; and frameless because she did not raise her hands to hold it.

'It's wonderful,' she said, shaking her head. 'They're lucky people.'

'They're relatives of mine. I first came here in 1938, before you were born. We used to have tea on the terrace and that year everybody was singing "There's a small hotel near a wishing well". We used to have a portable gramophone in those days.'

'And you always come back, don't you? You always come back to some place that you've been happy.'

He looked at her, wondering as always at her youth and inexperience.

'Yes,' he said with the passion one can only bring to an untruth, 'one always comes back.'

She stood for a few moments looking out over the lawn.

'Would you like to see the house?' he said.

'Oh, yes. It's a lovely house.'

'But we mustn't come here together again. Not I mean in my car.'

'I know,' she said, suddenly serious. 'I'll walk from the bus-stop.'

He took her arm and led the way to the side where the main door was. Inside it smelt dusty and dry like old wood: the scent of an empty house battened down against a series of hot rainless days. In the doorway of the drawing-room she stopped with her hands clasped awkwardly behind her back.

'Let's pull up the blinds. What a lovely room! Look at the pictures. And could we take off some of the dust-covers? I'm sure the furniture is beautiful.'

She plucked at a dust-cover that transformed an armchair into a shapeless half-human figure, crouching in the dim light.

'No,' he said, laying a hand on her arm.

She began to walk about the room peering at the shadowy paintings, the photographs on the side-tables, the silver bowl that stood in a heap of withered rose-leaves on top of the marble fireplace. She picked up one of the dry leaves and held it in her hand: it fell apart within her cupped palm like old parchment exposed to light.

'Philip, why didn't they take out the roses before they went away? They're all withered.' But when she looked around he was no longer in the room.

'Philip,' she called, 'Philip, where are you?'

She hurried out of the room, and blundered into the dining-room across the hall, into the breakfast-room behind, down the four steps into the pantry where the white enamel saucepans gleamed like skulls on the shelf.

'Philip!' She fought back a hysterical urge to scream as she ran back into the hall, and looked up the staircase. The return was a gloomy recess that wavered a little before her straining eyes; but light from the landing above flickered across the banisters and picked out the glass of the pictures that lined the wall, making them look like tiny windows in the dawn. Slowly she began to mount the stairs.

Philip O'Connor was standing at the end of the landing in front of a window looking down on the garden. He had opened the shutters; and the unexpected light blinded the girl as she came round the angle of the stairs, so that she could only see the dark outline of his slight figure against the shining casement.

'Is that you, Caroline?' he said, without turning round.

Caroline paused and leaned against the banister, feeling her heart thumping against the smooth wood. But when he turned towards her and held out his hand there was no hint of panic in her bearing as she crossed the landing and went to him. Instead there was a slight exaggeration of the *gaucherie*, the awkwardness with which two months ago she had first attracted him. Now for the first time, and instinctively, she used it to cover her fright.

He watched her with a smile as she came towards him with the light full upon her face.

'I heard you calling.' He took her arm and drew her close to him. 'Were you frightened?' He held her chin in his hand and looked searchingly into her eyes. But the look which met him was wide, blank and unafraid.

'No,' she said calmly. 'I just wondered what you were doing. Why are you standing here staring down like that?'

'You're growing up, my Caroline.' He put his hands on her shoulders and kissed her; firmly now and insistently as never before. It was as if he understood that their relationship had changed in some subtle way: a relationship which had been based on her innocent shamelessness, on his watchful passivity. At length he released her and began to close the shutters. The peacock blue of the bay was blocked from her sight by his back and his outspread arms. He turned round to darkness.

'The summer is not good for us,' he said in a low voice.

She crossed her arms and held them tightly across her breast.

'Shall we come back here again?' she asked.

He opened one of the doors leading off the landing, and beckoned to her. A shadow moved in a dim looking-glass on a dressing-table in the corner of the room as she went to him.

'Yes, Caroline, we shall always come back here.'

4

Mr Quill had married young—for an Irishman. He met Sybil Hennessy at a Sacred Heart sodality dance; and left her home when he discovered that she came from the same small town in the midlands as himself. She was some years older than he—ten in fact, although he never found it out—and had left the town to work in Dublin while he was still a boy; but she knew all the people that he knew, and kept up with the local gossip. Mr Quill was lonely; Sybil was desperate: and when, two years after they had begun to walk out, she inherited five thousand pounds from an uncle in Australia, she proposed to him. Mr Quill accepted her; and settled down in the small red-brick house in Sandycove which she had bought with part of the money. A year later Caroline was born.

During those war years Mr Quill went to his office every morning on the tram; and came home the same way in the afternoon. Caroline grew up and began to go to school. Her father did a little gardening; a little drinking in the evening; a little praying on Sundays and holy-days. Once a year they went to Galway for a fortnight, stopping on the way to visit their relations. Sybil was proud to be seen in public with such a handsome husband when the country was swarming with spinsters; Mr Quill was happy to have somebody to cook for him and darn his socks: they both loved Caroline.

Little by little the legacy disappeared: on furniture, on clothes, on Sybil's operation for womb trouble, on keeping up with the rising cost of living. Soon they were reduced to existing on Mr Quill's salary as a civil servant. But he was not an efficient clerk; he had no political friends in high places; no relations in the church: his promotion was slow. His salary was adequate for a small family living carefully in a small house with small pleasures and no social ambitions. There was enough to buy food, educate Caroline at a day-school, and purchase the necessary underclothing for the long Irish winter during the January sales. But Sybil was a bad manager. In 1944 five thousand pounds was a large sum of money in Ireland, and to the Quills, who had never possessed a penny of capital in their lives, it seemed as though it would never come to an end. But it did.

Mr Quill did not indulge in any complicated schemes to make more money. He did not bet on horses. He did not play the stock-market. He did not buy large quantities of Sweep tickets. He contributed a few shillings a week to one of Paul's raffles. Sybil did nothing at all. They simply went on living in the same way they had become accustomed to during the seven or eight years the legacy lasted. As the capital shrank, the glamour of it grew. It seemed to Sybil that she had been an heiress basking in the sun of fifty thousand instead of living in the half-shade of five.

The sanctity of its memory made it imperative to go on living as if they still had it: in this way it seemed to be always with them. Mr Quill continued to have his suits made by a good tailor in the city; Sybil refused to stand in queues at the cut-price grocery stores with the wives of other Government clerks. Mr Quill did not cut down on his smoking or drinking; it never entered Sybil's head to attend the sales or sit in the cheap seats at the cinema. They ran up bills everywhere. When tradesmen became pressing Sybil expressed horror and threatened to take her custom elsewhere. It is a fact that tradesmen are more willing to go on supplying a customer who owes them money in the hope of recovering it than to close the account and see them take their debts to a rival. By paying out small sums on account Sybil discovered that she received better attention than she had ever done when she was able to pay promptly. Or so she thought. There comes a time when even the most cautious shopkeepers will invoke the law.

Only in the matter of a car were the Quills unable to keep up an appearance of their former glory. They had not the capital it would take to buy a new one. But they often talked about it.

On the evening after the old Ford had broken down Sybil brought it up again. She had listened patiently and with complete indifference while her husband gave a long and complicated explanation of why he had to wait until midnight for a mechanic who had never turned up. Sybil believed every single word her husband told her. This was easy for her since she rarely listened to him. And in the case of the old Ford the more outrageous the adventures related—to these she gave half an ear—the more she agreed since it emphasized the social stigma of owning such a car. This stigma she was never tired of bemoaning. The fact that they could not possibly afford a new one did not stop her. The Quills never mentioned the lost legacy.

'Well,' said Sybil as she poured herself another cup of

tea, 'I see you managed to get the old crock home just the same. It's awful to see it in front of the house with everybody else having a new car in front of theirs.'

The dining-room was small, and Mr Quill's huge bulk made it seem smaller still. The three pieces of silver on the sideboard tinkled as he pushed back his chair and rose to his feet.

'It's all right. Some people get fond of a car. They keep it for sentimental reasons.'

'Miss Blake has a lovely new Rover.'

Mr Quill stood looking out of the window, darkening the light.

'Look at the Abbertons,' he said. 'They have a Rolls for forty years, and they wouldn't change it for anything.'

'Mrs Abberton was at Miss Blake's last night. She's an awfully nice person, so simple and unassuming, not like some of the ones in this terrace with their airs and graces.'

'I suppose I ought to mow the lawn.' Mr Quill peered out at the small patch of green in the back garden, and sighed. 'It would be nice if we had some standard roses under the window.'

'All the same the Triumph is a nice sort of a car. I often thought we ought to buy one of them.' Sybil nibbled at a piece of toast, and stared dreamily in front of her.

'Do you think it'll rain, Sybil? There's no point in starting to mow the lawn if it's going to rain.' A few wisps of cloud, remote and dreamy like stationary swans, floated in the glassy sky.

'Mrs Ryan next door—' Sybil broke off and brought down her cup with a little angry bang on the saucer. 'Do you know what that one said to me this morning. "Aren't you great," says she, "to spend so much time with poor old Miss Blake. I hear you do all her letters for her, as well as everything else. Is it that she's too mean to pay a companion?" Well of course the minute I heard that I knew what was up with her. Pure solid jealousy.'

Her husband came back and sat down again, pouring himself out a cup of lukewarm tea for want of something better to do. He was a little worried this evening. Paul had not been in Mick's when he was coming home. This happened so rarely that Mr Quill wondered if he was sick. He thought he might drop in again before closing time.

'The car I'd really like is a Mercedes,' he said. 'Like Philip has. They're the real thing.'

'As if,' went on Sybil, 'anything I did for poor Miss Blake wasn't done out of pure solid friendship. She often says to me "Sybil," she says, "you're the only friend I've got." Now isn't that nice ? There isn't one of the women in this terrace wouldn't go crawling up Miss Blake's avenue on their hands and knees if she invited them to tea. And the simple way I met her on the top of a tram. But she took to me at once. I bet some of the others were often sitting on the top of a tram with her but she didn't make friends with them. And the simple way it started, her not having enough money to pay the fare, a pure forget of course, and I having the amount in coppers. And the nice way she called on me to pay it back. It just goes to show you. Strange isn't it the way you meet people ? If it hadn't been for the war Miss Blake would never be sitting on the top of a tram. And then to hear that Ryan one saying that she heard she's as mean as cat's meat. Do you want another cup of tea ?'

Mr Quill rose from the table a second time accompanied by the usual tinkle of silver. He straightened a Paul Henry reproduction which hung over the fireplace, and which every evening was discovered by Mr Quill to be a fraction of an inch out of line.

'No, thanks. I think I'll go down to the sea for a bit of a walk. All this sitting in the office and driving a car isn't good for me. I've got no appetite and I'm beginning to lose weight.'

He prodded the large bunch of artificial gladioli on the hearth with his knee. Sybil always put them in front of the

26

empty grate in their cut-glass vase—a relic of the legacy—whenever she cleared the table for a meal.

'Mrs Abberton asked me to walk through her gardens any time I like.' Sybil stood up and began to collect the tea things on a tray. 'And do you know I think I will. We took to each other at once. I remember seeing a write-up about her garden in *Social and Personal* a few years ago But I don't know what way my hair is.'

'It's a funny thing we live only a few minutes from the sea and I never seem to go down to it. Look at all the men that go swimming every morning summer and winter in the Forty Foot. It gives you a great appetite for your food. If I took a swim I wouldn't be losing weight.'

'The rhododendrons will be out now,' said Sybil, studying her reflection in the fake Chippendale mirror over the sideboard—both relics of the legacy. 'I might be able to get a cutting for the garden. Rhododendrons would be lovely all banked at the bottom of our garden. Nobody else in the terrace has them.'

'How is it Caroline isn't home for her tea?'

'What's that?'

'I said Caroline—'

'Oh, Caroline, yes. Some of the tennis-club crowd asked her to tea. Such nice people she meets at the tennis-club. Very nice mixing, all Protestants.' Like many Irish Catholics Sybil was convinced that her Church of Ireland compatriots had a great deal less hope of getting to heaven than she; but she was equally convinced that they were socially superior, more honest, and more reliable than her Catholic neighbours.

Mr Quill also held this view. While his daughter was having tea with Protestants he knew no harm would come to her.

'What about the garden?' asked Sybil as her husband moved to the door.

'It's a pity to waste a fine evening like this when I could

be walking by the sea. God knows what sort of weather we'll have tomorrow.'

'It's beautiful weather for a garden, just ideal.' Sybil started out of the window. 'There's nothing as grand as rhododendrons. And roses. Miss Blake's roses are famous, did you know that?'

'It's too good.' Mr Quill backed into the hall. 'I'd be a blob in two minutes. I've lost enough weight as it is.'

'What do you mean it's too good?' said Sybil, following him into the hall and pushing open the kitchen door with her shoulder. 'I think I'll wear my linen suit, you know the one I got in Switzers.'

'Surely to God you're not going to mow the lawn and in your linen suit too,' burst out Mr Quill with his hand on the latch of the front door.

Sybil turned back from the kitchen and peered up at her husband with a frown. Like many women who marry men younger than themselves she did not look her age. Her daughter was very like her, except that Caroline had inherited some of her father's height. With age Sybil's long, somewhat irregular features had not hardened, nor did her dark-brown hair show more than a trace of grey. But her skin, which had never been fine, had roughened; and the angular coltish grace which she had passed on to Caroline had become exaggerated, so that it sometimes seemed as if all her limbs worked independently of one another. She had nothing of her husband's neatness, his physical dignity, his slow animal grace.

'I wish to God, John,' she said irritably, 'that you'd sometimes listen to what I have to say, God knows I don't talk about myself much, but I told you fifty times if I told you once that Mrs Abberton told me that I could walk through her garden. I didn't mean I was going to mow the lawn in my linen costume. I never heard of such a thing.'

'Oh, I thought—' said Mr Quill from the doorstep. 'Well, I mean I wouldn't want to have you mowing the lawn.'

Sybil's face softened, and she patted her hair.

'Go for a good walk, John, and have a drink for yourself. But don't overdo it. I distinctly noticed it recently that you're putting on weight.'

5

IRIS LEE looked up from her evening paper and found the man who had just come in staring at her. She put down her paper and stared back. The man did not lower his eyes, but looked boldly at the chair beside her. Miss Lee flung one gleaming knee across the other, took up her gin and tonic and opened her eyes very wide over its rim. Then the man walked past, a little unwillingly it seemed to her, and went over to the bar. Iris moved a little in her chair and stared after him.

Mr Quill approached the bar with something less than his usual aplomb. He had never become intimate with the other habitués of Mick's, except to nod vaguely to them as he passed in and out. Their faces, like their conversation, were part of the blurred background against which he and Paul had stood out in bold relief, secure in their ten-year place inside the door. He felt a trifle disconcerted. He ordered the usual, and glanced a little uncertainly at the man beside him. His face, like most of the others, was vaguely familiar. But before he could summon up enough courage to ask the question which was troubling him, the man anticipated him.

'No Paul tonight,' he said out of the corner of his mouth, without turning his head.

'No.' Mr Quill leaned his elbow on the counter and looked across at the strange woman who was sitting on the hallowed chair. At this distance her face was blurred, and although he could see that she was staring at the bar, he could not be sure that she was looking at him.

'What's up?' said the man.

Mr Quill hesitated. He did not want to give the impression that he had not the faintest idea of what had happened to Paul.

'Well. I know he wasn't feeling good these last few days. A little stomach upset or something.'

'I'm not surprised. A bottle of twelve-year-old every night. It's a wonder he isn't dead years ago.'

'Paul can carry his liquor,' said Mr Quill firmly. 'It was something he ate.'

'Food-poisoning.' The man wriggled his plump bottom on the bar-stool at the approach of a congenial topic. 'A neighbour of mine died of it a few months ago. Horrible.' He turned round, got down from his stool, adjusted it, looked at the woman in Paul's chair out of the corner of his eye, and then sat up again. 'Who's the tart over there? I wouldn't be surprised if she knew something about him.'

'Paul,' said Mr Quill, putting down his pint with a bang, 'is not interested in women.' That had been the pattern of their relationship. He was the man for the women.

'That's what you think,' said the man with a cynical snigger. 'Do you mean to tell me that he's wasting his time calling on all those houses during the afternoon with all the men away at work?'

Mr Quill was outraged. His ruddy face flushed deeper with anger, and a rich creamy blob of Guinness settled on his gleaming cuff as he took up his pint again with trembling hand to cover his confusion.

'Paul collects subscriptions. He has to call on dozens of houses every day—'

'Yes, collecting his shilling I don't think. It's little enough for what he gives them don't tell me.' The man looked at him out of the corner of his eyes, sandy-lashed to match his hair, and ran his tongue over his frothy lip. 'As if you didn't know.'

A great struggle raged in Mr Quill's breast. Jealousy, disbelief, amazement, and a kind of pleasure shot through his consciousness like a series of tiny electric shocks. The whole thing was of course a monstrous lie; yet he felt that to deny it would not only be a reflection on Paul, but also on their friendship. It would be impossible to confess that apart from the fact that he knew Paul lived somewhere at the back of the town, he knew nothing whatever about him. It was one of those bar-acquaintances, like the café-friendships of Spain, where anything more intimate than sex is never discussed.

'One man's raffle is another man's opportunity,' went on the red-haired man with relish. 'I wish I had thought of it. It's a right racket if you ask me. All that and heaven too. I bet he gives you some of his cards now and again. I wish he'd give one or two to me. I'd show them the biggest prize in Dublin, the best sixpenny dip they ever saw. Anyway, what'll you have?'

Although Miss Lee had been watching this encounter with interest, she could not hear it above the hum and buzz of the bar. But she felt justified in thinking that she was the subject of it. The way the big man kept staring at her for one thing. Then that old trick of sliding off the stool and looking at you from under his eyes that the red-haired one used. Miss Lee hadn't been born yesterday. And then for a moment it seemed as though they were having an argument about her. She sighed happily, and contemplated Mr Quill's profile with pleasure. He was just her type. Those great shoulders; that sensual mouth; the small vicious ears; the thick curling hair. She caught the barman's eye and raised her finger.

'I'll have the same again, dear,' she said with a brilliant smile. The barman, who was elderly and set in his ways, was not used to such smiles; nor was he used to ladies like Miss Lee. Mick's, like most Irish bars, was a man's bar; such women as frequented it were apt to be as old as the barman: shapeless figures in black who were not likely to distract the men from their serious conversation. The old man tottered off, a bit troubled in mind.

'I just got off the boat this morning,' she said when he came back with her drink. 'Such a crossing! I didn't know there were such boats in the world. I thought I'd die. But I slept all afternoon. And now I'm all set for my relations.'

'Your relations, ma'am.' The barman's white eyebrows shot up.

'Yes, dear. I'm just as Irish as you are, although I've been across the water for some years. You wouldn't think it, would you?'

The barman looked at Miss Lee's smooth golden curls, her fluttering eyelashes, her plump but well-controlled bust, her long shining legs, and blinked noncommittally.

'First time I've been home for years, dear, but you get a longing to come back to the old country, don't you? Of course I haven't any near relations, except a crummy old uncle somewhere about here, Mummy and Daddy died when I was a kid. An only child too, dear, all alone in the world. But I have scads of cousins all living round here. Who's that big man over there, dear? He looks like a first cousin of mine. The big man with the black hair.'

'Is it Mr Quill? He wouldn't be a cousin of yours, he's from down the country.'

'I have country cousins too, dear,' said Miss Lee. 'Why I ask is that he keeps on looking at me as if he thinks he's seen me before, too.'

'Oh, is that what you mean, the way he's looking at you? I wouldn't think there's any blood in that. It's only that you're sitting in his friend's chair.'

'His friend,' said Miss Lee sharply.

'Yes. First night he's missed here for the past ten years. They always sit at this table. That's what he's looking at. He's wondering about his friend. I hope he's not sick, a real nice gentleman, one of our best customers. Will that be all, ma'am?'

Miss Lee nodded and the barman ambled off. For a moment a horrid suspicion assailed her; and she looked keenly at the other habitués of the place. Then she relaxed and picked up her drink. No, it was clearly not that sort of bar; nor did Mr Quill look like that sort of man. Of course Miss Lee knew that a girl could never be sure: she had had some shocks in her time. And then, just as she was wondering what she ought to do, she saw Mr Quill turn towards her, his heavy eyelids half-closed, his mouth curved in a suggestive smile.

'Ah, no,' he was saying, 'people exaggerate you know. Of course I don't say that Paul doesn't have his little bit of fun now and again like any man. But I wouldn't say he's much good on his own. I know him very well, and I can tell you that he's a shy sort of a man. In fact I often had to fix him up with something in that line myself.'

'Go away,' said the man, who was on his sixth Guinness, and full of amazement.

Mr Quill's eyes grew heavier still, and the dimples on either side of his mouth deepened.

'Yes, indeed. Of course we don't go in for the same type. I prefer something with a little more class myself. Paul doesn't care, a woman is just a woman to him.'

'I bet. You're a deep one you are. I always thought it to look at you. What way do you like it ?' He finished off his pint, and coiled one of his ankles round the leg of the stool.

'This one is on me,' said Mr Quill, turning back to the bar.

'Excuse me,' said Miss Lee, putting down her empty glass on the counter between the two men. 'I want to order another drink.'

Mr Quill's neighbour leaned away so violently on his stool that he had to clasp the counter for support, while Mr Quill himself pressed back against the end-wall of the bar and looked at the lady with eyes suddenly bright, hard, and suspicious. Miss Lee found herself alone in a little oasis sufficient to give space to three men.

'A little bird told me I've been sitting in your chair,' she said archly, turning her back to the man on the stool, and flashing her brilliant smile in Mr Quill's direction.

'It's quite all right, ma'am, quite all right.'

Miss Lee paid for her drink and raised it to her lips.

'Cheers.' Then her eyes, which had been regarding her own image in the mirror behind the bar, suddenly opened as wide as flapjacks, and she gave a little gasp. A man had just come in; a little man with stiff grey hair, and a long nose on the end of which a large pimple blazed.

'Well, for heaven's sake,' cried Miss Lee, turning round and running to him to throw her arms about his neck, 'if it isn't Uncle Paul.'

6

MR QUILL paused inside the gates of Philip O'Connor's house listening to the little tapping sound behind the empty gate-lodge. The great beeches and chestnuts lining the avenue were as silent as himself in the sultry evening sun. As gently as an African stalking game, he made his way through the shrubbery at the side of the lodge and came out into the open space at the back. Mr Quill took out his spectacles and peered under one of the chestnut trees where the sound came from. A thrush was battering a snail against a stone. He watched the deadly game for a few seconds and then clapped his hands. There was a flutter of spider-like claws, a rustle of leaves, and then silence. He looked at the stone where the bird had been killing her prey. But he could see nothing. He was too late. He stepped back and looked up at the chestnut, serene and heedless in its summer glory. A few months ago in the spring he had stood under it when the buds had been like damp fists pointing at the sky. Then on a later visit the fists had unclenched, and the huge hand-like leaves pointed heavenwards like a gesticulating crowd.

'Oh, hullo. I wondered who it was. How are you, Mr Quill?'

Mr Quill, whose gestures became sharper and more accurate when he was wearing his spectacles, spun round. A tall slim woman wearing yellow slacks stepped out from behind the shrubbery. She was followed by two tiny dogs with huge solemn eyes, and flat muzzles moustached and whiskered like old men. They cocked their heads sideways and gazed at Mr Quill thoughtfully.

'Good evening Mrs O'Connor. I was just—'

'Yes, I know, I heard it too. I suppose one can't really feel anything about snails, but then I have never cared for birds. Horrid selfish little things, I always think. The only time I feel anything about them is when I see the cats stalking them. Look, Tubby and Muff remember you.'

The little dogs had walked gingerly forward, sniffed the bottom of Mr Quill's trousers, and after a discreet interlude wagged their stumpy tails. Mr Quill got down on his hunkers, and held out the back of his hand to them in the manner of a bishop humbly giving his ring to be kissed. One of them licked his knuckles delicately, while the other sat back and looked up at him quizzically.

Mrs O'Connor laughed, a surprisingly throaty chuckle, which never failed to disconcert people who had been put off by her high cool voice.

'Muff is a flatterer, but Tubby has nothing to conceal,' she said.

Mr Quill stroked the top of Tubby's quiet little head, while Muff the ardent and flattering one frisked about his feet.

'What's this breed they are, I can never remember?'

'Belgian griffons. They're quite rare in this country. Children think they're monkeys, and one old woman blessed herself when she saw them. They do look startlingly human, don't they?'

Again the curious, almost ribald chuckle. Mr Quill looked up and smiled at the tall horse-faced woman with the periwinkle-blue eyes, and the nervous trick of smiling with one corner of her mouth. He had always felt at ease with Philip's English wife. In spite of the clear self-confident accent, the tone of which always arouses atavistic instincts of inferiority in every Irish person, Lilian O'Connor had never intimidated him. He had no sense with her of that language of the blood beyond the sound of words which makes intercourse between Irish people a sort of conversational Chinese puzzle. The luxury of saying what one means as distinct from making an impression is an imperial heritage.

'I suppose you've come to see Philip.'

'Is he in?'

'Of course. He's expecting you.' Lilian gave her jerky smile and turned away. 'Let's walk back this way.'

Mr Quill followed her and the two dogs through the grove of beech and chestnut between the wide curve of the avenue. They walked across the meadow beyond which on rising ground the house stood: a square Regency lodge, with gleaming bow-windows, pretty iron balconies painted white, and high ornamental chimneys. Behind the shrubbery at the edge of the sloping lawn, the pink bricks of the walled garden rose against a sky which gleamed like newly washed bone china. When Mr Quill thought of Philip's house it seemed to him that the sun always shone on it. He had a muddled feeling, which he did not find unpleasant, that the rich can also command the elements.

He followed Lilian as she climbed the slope from the meadow on to the gravel in front of the house. He had always been struck by the way she walked, thinking that it reminded him of somebody he knew. The fact that she was twenty years older, that she was English and rich and the mother of two children, made it impossible for him to recognise in that slightly awkward gait, in that coltish grace the resemblance between her and his own daughter. But the half-conscious recognition of something dear and familiar made him feel more than ever at ease with this woman, making their relationship at once vivid and remote.

'There's Philip,' said Lilian. 'I'll leave you two alone. I've got to give these little people their walk.' With a jerky wave of her arm, a sudden puppet-like gesture as if her hands had been lifted into the air by invisible strings, she turned back down the avenue with the griffons.

Philip stood at the open door, smiling. Mr Quill felt a sudden pang of blind terror. It was not only the nature of his visit which made him nervous: he had always been like that with Philip. They had known each other all their lives; and the pattern of their relationship had been formed long ago in the country town in the midlands where they were born.

Mr Quill's father had been a policeman, first in the old Royal Irish Constabulary, and after the Treaty a sergeant in the new Civic Guards. He died in early middle-age and his widow was left to rear a family of eight on a tiny pension which she augmented by dressmaking. Life was hard, but it was not unhappy. Mrs Quill, a tiny woman of strong will and endless vitality, was not given to complaining; deeply religious, she taught her children that the world in spite of poverty and hardship and sickness was a good place to live in. She handed on to them the gift of laughter, and the somewhat more doubtful legacy of a boundless optimism. It was this vital acceptance of the passing moment, together with his animal high spirits, which first drew Philip O'Connor, lonely, shy, and inhibited, to the big red-faced schoolboy whose clothes were always too tight for his huge limbs, at the convent school which they both attended from their fourth to their eighth year.

Social distinctions are vague in Ireland; but there are certain subtle and stubborn barriers. The O'Connors were rich; had been rich for three generations from a chain of drapery shops in the larger midland towns. They had also acquired all the respectable vices of the Irish bourgeoisie during the reign of Queen Victoria. They were snobbish, purse-proud, and devoid of enthusiasm. Any display of natural buoyancy, except within strictly defined limits designed to conceal rather than express real feelings, was regarded as dangerous bad taste. Their whole life was permeated with a profound and largely unconscious hypocrisy. Money was the only god they worshipped; although, pious and bigoted Catholics as they were they would have been horrified if anybody had told them so. They knew that money could only be kept and increased by thrift, caution, and lack of ostentation: their religion was an outward manifestation of these principles. Honest, hardworking, frugal, sexless, hating every exhibition of emotion, they possessed all the virtues which cost nothing to maintain.

But they were strangers in a strange land: a race of people that had never existed in Ireland before the nineteenth century. They were the gombeen men, who had modelled themselves on the rising industrial class in England. Their immediate ancestors had been peasants: disinherited men with a dream of past glory, a sense of poetry, and no knowledge of middle-class respectability. There was a bawdy medieval spirit lurking in their withered souls. It broke out, showing itself in strange twisted forms, once or twice in every generation. Doomed from birth, reared to values foreign to their nature, these sons and daughters of bombazine respectability grew up with an alien sense of shame. It was Philip O'Connor's tragedy that he was born with an eighteenth-century mind and an embarrassing sense of beauty.

The O'Connors did not approve of their son's friendship with young Quill. But in time they relented. Mrs Quill was noted for all the virtues which they admired. She was poor—a disease they detested—but she was respectable.

And she did sewing for Philip's mother. That clinched it. The O'Connors were incapable of understanding any human relationship which they did not in some way control. John Quill was certainly not an ideal companion for Philip; but he would keep him from worse; and if he did not behave himself according to Mrs O'Connor's standards he could be reprimanded through his mother. So it came to pass that the two little boys spent all of their free time playing in the large prim garden of Philip's house.

Gradually the house and its occupants reversed the natural balance of friendship between the children. Philip at home was quite different from the lonely little boy in the convent yard. He was used to having his own way: he was quick-witted, sharp-tongued, and oblique. He was emotionally self-reliant and physically helpless like so many only children of rich elderly parents. John Quill soon realized that his great strength, which had made him master of the convent playground, and which he had used out of sheer good nature to defend the helpless little boy who was to become his friend, was of little avail once he was inside the gates of Philip's house.

He was made to realize in a hundred little ways, by Philip and his parents—especially by Philip, who could never forget the indignity of having to be rescued from a naked force which he could not control—that he was clumsy, slow-witted, and poor. Above all that he was poor. Gradually the clever graceful little boy, who preferred the novels of Walter Scott to robbing birds' nests, achieved a complete mental hegemony over his good-natured companion. John Quill lost faith in the only natural gift providence had bestowed on him—his splendid physique. When Philip began giving part of his pocket-money to his penniless friend the rout was complete; the pattern formed.

It was a pattern which imposed itself again when the two met in Dublin as adults. Although Philip's parents had died; although he had started a successful clothing factory in Dublin, come to live in the capital, married and become a father, they slipped easily into their old child-hood relationship. Philip still called the tune; and John Quill danced, as the helpless are always glad to do.

7

'WELL, John, what'll you have?' Philip lifted the bottle of brandy from the tray, and tapped the neck with his finger-nail. Philip always drank brandy.

'Whatever you're having, Philip.' Mr Quill had no objection to brandy, but he had never summoned up enough courage to ask for water with it. Philip poured out the glasses, and handed one to his visitor.

'Ginger?'

'Thanks, Philip. Not too much for me, please.'

Philip straightened up and looked at his friend with a frown.

'You don't have to have ginger if you don't want it.'

'Well—' Mr Quill cleared his throat.

'Oh, for heaven's sake, John, stop being polite. If you want water ask for water. If you want it neat take it neat. Has anybody ever changed less in thirty-years? Do you remember taking sugar in your tea just because we all took it? And stirring it too. If your mother hadn't mentioned it to Daddy we'd never have known. Here's the water.'

'Lovely brandy this.' Mr Quill sniffed his glass.

Philip, who had gone to the window, spun round.

'I bet you don't like brandy either. I bet that all these years—'

'Oh, no, no, Philip, I love brandy. It's just that I don't get the chance of it often. At least not old brandy like this.'

'It isn't old brandy, and if you want whiskey you can have it.'

'I'm telling you that I like this brandy,' said Mr Quill with some heat.

Philip came back from the window and sat down on a high chair opposite his friend. He looked at him closely for a few moments, his fore-finger pressed judicially against his nose.

'When did you start wearing glasses?' he asked suddenly.

Mr Quill fumbled with his spectacles, folding them with one hand, and stuffing them into his pocket. At once the clean severe outlines of Philip's white-walled study blurred and smudged like damp paint brushed across a canvas with a careless elbow. Mr Quill had been thinking how extraordinary it was that anybody as rich as Philip should work in such a bare room, with its block floor polished like a convent parlour. No pictures, no flowers, no heavy velvet hangings, no plump coloured cushions. And that smell of old leather books. In his opinion a couple of thousand books were not enough to furnish any room.

'I don't wear them. At least not all the time. I'm a little short-sighted, all that office-work I suppose. I only wear them for writing and driving. I forgot to take them off.'

'You used to have good sight,' said Philip, almost accusingly.

Mr Quill had never had perfect vision; but he had not discovered this until he went into the Civil Service. When he ran into his old friend again, ten years ago in Grafton Street, he had not been wearing them, and he had always taken them off whenever he called on Philip since.

'Well, I'm thirty years older now,' he said sadly.

'But are you thirty years wiser, John?' Philip gave his deep mirthless little laugh.

Mr Quill flushed and put down his drink.

'Listen, Philip,' he blurted out, 'I haven't the money to pay you back.'

'Haven't you?' Philip's voice was noncommittal. He seemed not to be paying much attention. He sat looking down thoughtfully at his brandy which moved in Mr Quill's vision like a swaying goldfish.

'I'm awfully sorry, Philip. I haven't got it. Honest.'

'It doesn't matter,' said Philip lightly. 'Do you want any more?'

Mr Quill was so surprised and relieved that he did something he had never done with another human being: he took out his spectacles and stared. But Philip was not looking. He was looking away, his profile etched against the bright window behind. Mr Quill was assailed by a confusion of thoughts and emotions. He had not looked at Philip so closely, or seen him so clearly for many years. With the light behind blacking out the shadows and the lines about the eyes and mouth, he seemed hardly changed at all. Whenever Mr Quill remembered his friend it was like this: with his neat, coin-like profile and his well-shaped head tilted sideways, always polite, self-assured and remote. One never remembered him leaning forward full-faced giving his enthusiastic attention. And he had always disposed of problems lightly. For three months Mr Quill had been worrying about this interview; knowing that he couldn't possibly get together the seventy pounds he had borrowed. The crisis had been brought about by a solicitor's letter from the grocer to Mr Quill personally.

'Oh, no, Philip, I don't want any more. It's just that I haven't been able to get it in such a short time. I'll pay you back by the end of the year.'

'It doesn't matter,' said Philip in the same careless tone. 'Don't worry about it. If you find yourself in trouble again let me know.'

Mr Quill took off his spectacles, blinked and stared into his brandy. Suddenly Philip started up and began to tug his collar with his thumb and forefinger.

'Look,' he exlaimed in a passionate voice, 'look at that

collar. I bought half-a-dozen silk shirts a few months ago, and one by one they've been ruined in the laundry. Every time Lilian sends out a message, and we've spent a fortune on telephone calls, and every time they come back starched. Starched!' He looked down with wide angry eyes, still clutching his collar with one hand and pointing his brandy glass at Mr Quill with the other. 'Do you know I shall have to wash my shirts myself. I've got to do everything myself. You can't get anybody to do anything any more. Oh, God, it's awful!'

Mr Quill bore this outburst calmly. Philip had always fussed about trifles. While he could face a threatened strike, or the arrival of a new and dangerous business rival, with cool detachment, a book put back into the wrong place on the shelf, a flower torn up and trampled on its bed, a mislaid magazine, caused him to fly into a rage.

'Well, you know, Philip, you can afford ten dozen shirts, all silk, and at wholesale price too, if you want,' said Mr Quill quietly.

Philip glared at him; but he had begun to be mollified. His flashes of irritation never lasted long; nervous spasms, they wore themselves out, especially if they met with firm treatment. Like most men who have taken on responsibility early in life and succeeded in it, Philip had a deep unconfessed craving to have his mind made up for him sometimes by somebody else.

'It isn't that,' he said in a quieter voice. 'It's the hopeless inefficiency of it, the awful apathy. How on earth have we persuaded ourselves that this is the most efficient century since the world began? It isn't. It's just the opposite. Try and get yourself even the minimum of decent service in any shop, or in any hotel or restaurant, and you can't. Try and get a licence from the Government. Oh, just try and get anything done. Do you know that I've never yet travelled on a 'plane that left on time or got in on time. And if you say this to people they just stare at you as if you were mad. They've been told that the airlines are

43

efficient, and they believe it like the Pilgrim Fathers believed the Bible.'

'I've never been in a 'plane,' said Mr Quill with all his old boyish eagerness. 'It must be great.'

Philip stopped and stared at his friend in perplexity; then his tense expression softened.

'Good old John,' he murmured affectionately. 'You haven't changed.' Then he poured out another two drinks, and announced that they were for the road, since he had work to do.

When Mr Quill left the house he was humming to himself, flushed with brandy and success. He pulled a flaming red bloom from a clump of rhododendrons inside the gate, and threw it up into the air like a coloured ball. Then he walked out on to the road holding the bloom in his hand, provoking an embarrassed giggle from a couple of Teddy-boys passing by who were unaccustomed to seeing a large, soberly-dressed man of mature years regarding a flowering shrub as if it were a new toy. But Mr Quill did not hear them. He was too hopeful.

Philip O'Connor lived in Glenageary, a mile or two from Mr Quill, and when he went to call he always parked his car a hundred yards down the road for fear his rich friend should see how old and battered it was. When he reached it he stood for a few minutes under the shade of a laburnum whose fading blossoms spattered his face and neck like flakes from a mouldering ceiling. Far off a church bell rang, and Mr Quill instinctively blessed himself, having lost count of time, and thinking it was the Angelus. As he raised his hand to his forehead the Rhododendron bloom fell from his fingers, and lay among the blossoms of the laburnum like a red shoe in a pool of petticoats. As he finished his prayer he looked at his watch. Nine o'clock. Mr Quill sighed happily. Two-and-a-half hours' drinking time. No hurry. He got into the car and drove along the road and chugged up Dalkey Hill.

Dublin lay spread out under him in a golden evening

haze, its roofs, towers and domes seeming to flicker and bend sideways, in Mr Quill's vision, like a scene glimpsed in a driving-mirror of a speeding car. The light dipped and swayed over the flickering roofs like a flock of birds floating in the eastern sky at dawn. But already the great bay below was being invaded by dark blue shadows from the east: they splayed out from the horizon, an armada of fishing boats making for the harbour at the end of the day, dragging night in their nets. Howth Head was already streaked with violet, and looked to Mr Quill like a basking whale in the far waters. So many wonders for him to see that to another would be merely a famous view taken out of its frame in a postcard.

But his mood was beginning to change, especially since nothing contributes to a thirst like a sublime motion. Besides he wanted to share his happiness with his friends. So he started up the old Ford and sped down the hill in neutral to Mick's.

8

'WHAT did you say her name was?' said Miss Lee.

'No names, no, well, whatever it is,' said Mr Quill.

'Her name was Mary,' sang Paul softly, his eyelids drooping maliciously, as he looked from his friend to his niece over his whiskey.

'Dublin,' commented Miss Lee with a pretty pout, 'must be a right place. I never heard of such goings-on.'

'A blight race,' said Paul.

'Mind you,' said Mr Quill, 'I only said I brought her up to Dalkey Hill for a spin.'

'Oh, ho,' said Paul, raising himself and turning his book.

'What are you reading anyway?' said his niece. 'You're always reading something. Is it banned?'

'*The Private Life of Queen Victoria*. A rare book, published in 1839. Traces her possible development as a woman in the light of her heredity. Makes some remarkable prophecies that never came true. So far as we know,' he concluded darkly.

'What did you do up that hill, that's what I want to know.' Miss Lee looked at Mr Quill's ripe red mouth, and allowed her drooping eyes to linger on his huge thighs, firmly outlined against his light summer-weight trousers as he bent back his legs and crossed his feet under his chair.

'Now, now, that's no question for a nice girl to ask. We went for a spin and looked at the view and came back again.'

'I'm not a nice girl.'

'And then came back again. She's a nice girl. Her uncle is a parish priest.'

'My round,' said Paul.

'It's nice to be home again,' said Miss Lee gloomily when her newly filled glass was placed in front of her. 'I knew I'd have a good time in Dublin.'

'We're all having a good time,' said Mr Quill. 'I never felt better in my life. Life is great.'

'This is the way to have a good time.' Paul inhaled the smell of his whiskey sensuously.

'We hear,' said Mr Quill, who was no longer in complete command of his tongue, 'that you have a good time in more ways than that. We hear that you don't hurry too much over your shilling collection.'

'Who told you that?' Paul grasped his bottle by the neck and banged it on the table. 'Tell me who told you that and I'll have him labelled for libel in the High Court, the dirty teetotaller. Who is he anyway?'

'No name, no, ah—' Mr Quill stopped agape, his mind slipping again from the cliché, like a drowning hand off a slimy rock.

'Pack-drill,' put in Miss Lee, holding out her hand palm uppermost, as if she were handing over the words.

'This is a lovely way to spend an evening,' said Mr Quill, sticking his thumbs in his braces and leaning back with a yawn, expanding his gleaming linen chest.

'Oh, God yes,' said Miss Lee with a sigh.

'I never drink when I'm on my rounds. If I did they'd smell it off me and try to pawn me off with a sixpence instead of a shilling. I'd like to know the dirty hound that's trying to ruin my good name with the clergy by telling you things like that.'

Mr Quill leaned forward and patted his old friend's arm. That slip of the tongue a few minutes ago was a near thing: it could have ruined the subtle balance of ten years. He was the man for the women. And, he reflected happily, everything was going well with him tonight.

'Don't mind them, Paul. It's just that they're jealous of all the subscribers you have, and all the money you win every week. I knew that the moment I heard it. Besides I only said it to rise you, honest I did.'

Paul pursed his lips in thought for a few seconds, and then tapped his glass on the table.

'Your round.'

Miss Lee, who was beginning to feel faintly sick, excused herself when she saw the new round arriving and made for the ladies' room. Inside, in the cracked mirror over the dirty hand-basin, she studied herself, and found much to admire in the smooth face with its creamy skin and its pouting pink lips; nor could she, even by bending forward and squinting into the glass, find any flaw in her plump and generously exposed bosom. She did not have to study her small waist, cunningly set off by the flared skirt of her silk dress, to know that she had not gained a single inch in that region over the past five years. The mirror was too high for her to admire her legs, so she bent down and looked at them, sleek, and shapely, and shining in their flesh-coloured nylon.

'What the hell does he want?' she murmured wonderingly to her image. 'I'm young, I'm pretty and I'm willing. Well maybe I'm thirty and a bit, but that's no age, and don't tell me that men don't like experience because they do and I ought to know.'

'Are you all right?' a wheezy voice said behind her. Miss Lee stared into the mirror with frightened eyes, and saw the bloated face with its wisps of yellow-white hair escaping from a black, shapeless hat. She gave the woman a startled glare and fled past her to the door. But it would not open. She tugged at it desperately for a few moments until she began to feel hysterical.

'Take it easy, my dear.' Miss Lee shrank back against the wall. A broad back, clothed in dusty black, bent over the door, and opened it gently. 'It gets stuck sometimes. You have to know the trick. Don't come in here often, do you?'

'No. Thank you. I must go.'

A plump yellow hand with black finger-nails was laid on her arm. Miss Lee was too frightened to notice that the woman was wearing a large emerald ring.

'Would you have a penny for the slot? No change on me tonight.'

Miss Lee fumbled in her bag, and located a penny stuck in an envelope.

'Thank you, my dear.' The black finger-nails touched her arm again. 'Penny-in-the-slot, penny-in-the-slot, that's what all the men think.'

Miss Lee jerked her arm away and stumbled out into the crowded bar, clawing her way past the closely tied knots of men who leaned forward on their toes balancing their pints expertly as she struggled by. When she got back to her seat she found that her hands were trembling and she had to grasp her glass firmly with both palms to raise it.

'A trull,' Paul was saying. 'Set them down for sluttish spoils of opportunity and daughters of the same.'

'This one is different. This one is a lady. Look at the wrists she has and the ankles and the fine silky hair and—'

'And the eye on the crotch. Different how are you.'

'When we got to the top of Dalkey Hill and she looked down at the view, do you know what she said?'

'She said is there any place we can sit down, that's what she said. My round.'

Mr Quill shook his head and gazed dreamily into space.

'Well, go on, what did she say?' said Miss Lee irritably.

But Mr Quill did not hear her. Paul was shouting for the barman.

'I don't want any more drink,' said Miss Lee faintly. The drink was brought. She yielded to the force of circumstance and drank deeply. There didn't seem much else to do.

'Is she a good lay?' Paul unbuttoned the top of his trousers and belched.

'Is she a good what?' said Mr Quill, frowning.

'I said is she good in the matters for which women are supposed to be famous, or is she like they all really are?'

'You haven't the right idea at all, Paul. This girl wants love and affection—'

'I know what you want, you old hypocrite. Come on now, is she or isn't she?'

'I don't say that in my time carried away by the forces of passion I haven't always acted as, ah, a man should.'

'What may I ask,' said Miss Lee, 'in the name of Almighty God does that mean?'

Mr Quill chuckled lasciviously.

'I'm an awful man, God help me, but I am. Not that I don't respect her as a man should.'

'Aw, you're just a randy old goat,' said Paul.

Mr Quill smiled and stretched his legs, running his small hands with their thick hairy wrists along his thighs. Miss Lee leaned forward on her folded arms, exposing her firm, blue-veined breasts to the view of all who might admire them. The two men went on talking about women: Paul cynical, but provocative: Mr Quill treading his way

49

delicately, as he did in all things, between the dry wood of the probable and the fiery furnace of the improbable. Miss Lee wriggled sideways in her chair and threw one leg over the other, pulling her skirts well up above her knee, and allowing the tip of her tiny shoe to touch the calf of Mr Quill's leg. She leaned forward even farther, cupping her breast in her hand. She insinuated the whole of her leg into a warmly provocative position alongside Mr Quill's. She could feel his well-developed calf, hard as a board against her silken limb. The two men went on talking about women. Mr Quill had once found romance in a railway carriage, again in a tram; in restaurants, cinemas, and windy western beaches during the Galway races. Beautiful, well-mannered girls with slim ankles and damask skin. Miss Lee's elbow slipped from the table and she grasped at his manly thigh for support, withdrawing the hold slowly and unwillingly as Mr Quill described the charms of a doctor's daughter who had climbed down the ivy on her father's house to wander with him in the moonlight. Miss Lee stood up and smoothed her dress into place, running her hands caressingly over her breasts, her waist and her hips. She yawned, exclaimed that she was tired sitting down, and leaned on the back of Mr Quill's chair allowing her bust to tickle his ear. The doctor's daughter went on wandering in the moonlight, looking at the stars.

Suddenly Paul stared up and held his hand against his chest, while his eyes roved wildly about the bar. It was a signal that Mr Quill knew well. Indeed so complete was their accord that he too began to feel sick. He rose with a grunt and took his old friend's arm, and they made their way with stiff-legged dignity to the lavatory. There side by side before the urinals they coughed and belched and vomited up most of what they had drunk. It was a happy, intimate occasion. Mr Quill was the first to recover. He leaned against the wall and wiped the foam of vomit from his mouth. Then he put his arm around Paul's shoulder to support him as he retched in the gathering slime below.

'That was a good night,' said Mr Quill happily. 'A right good night.'

'Jesus yes,' panted Paul, staggering back against the wall and fumbling with his fly. He couldn't manage it, so Mr Quill helped him. Never were two men greater friends.

Back in the bar Miss Lee felt that the multi-coloured walls were leaning forward and about to fall upon her. She groped on the ground for her coat and pulled it about her shivering shoulders. Suddenly out of the maze of tangled figures swaying like shadows in the smoky bar she saw a fat old woman in black waddling towards her. A yellow finger tapped her wrist heavily, the emerald gleaming dully in the dim light.

'Lost your gentlemen friends, have you, my dear? Well, that's the way it goes. So we all do in the end. Good night, and, oh, I forgot something. The penny that you lent me. Got some change since.'

Miss Lee, who had closed her eyes, opened them and saw the penny beside her half-empty glass of gin. She picked it up gingerly and threw it over her shoulder. Then she remembered that she wanted to pay another visit to the ladies' and was out of change. But the penny was not to be found, although she got down on her knees and scrabbled about on the floor for it. She got to her feet slowly, supporting herself with Mr Quill's chair. I wonder, she thought, is there anybody here who'd lend me one. It never occurred to her, any more than it ever does to ladies like Miss Lee, to ask the barman.

9

A SHAFT of sunlight pierced the mirror on the dressing-table from a chink in the drawn curtains. Caroline lay watching it for a long time, her body as light and lazily happy as the motes of dust that flickered in the gleaming ray of light. Then the shaft wavered, like a sword under water, and disappeared. The mirror clouded. Something of the physical exaltation, which possesses every woman after love-making seemed to leave her with the veiling of the sun. She turned and looked at the dim, coin-like profile which seemed carved on the pillow beside her, like an effigy on a tomb. The eyes were closed and the smooth marble chest was still. Only by leaning over him could she see the heart pulse under the curving ribs.

Very carefully, so as not to wake him, she raised her hands and touched her neck and breasts. Then lightly, with a certain timidity, she rested her finger-tip on the arm that lay in the hollow between their two bodies. Under the thick silken hair that covered the flesh she could feel the ebb and flow of the deep tidal wave of sleep that engulfed him. But the sleeper did not wake. She knew there was nothing for it but to wait until the carved profile flickered back into life, and brought with it some semblance of that unity which a few moments ago, more with her body than with her mind, she had discovered did not exist. The minutes ticked on on Philip's wrist-watch as she grew into the knowledge of solitude.

Suddenly he stirred and turned towards her, his eyes open, a tiny dribble of saliva dripping from the corner of his mouth. She bent down and touched it with her lips, licking his mouth dry with her tongue. He began to raise his arm, but she caught his wrist and held it firmly while she slipped her arm about his shoulders and drew his head on to her breast. Her body grew less wary as she rested her chin on his head; but her eyes flickered watchfully about the room.

'I didn't want to wake you,' she whispered. 'But I'm glad you have.'

'Weren't you thankful to be let alone?' he chuckled sleepily, kneading her breast with his cheek.

'No, no. I felt—I don't know how I felt.'

52

He raised himself from her embrace and held a finger under her chin.

'You felt alone.'

'No. Yes. Oh, Philip, yes.'

'You have grown up, my Caroline.'

She took his hand away from her chin and drew his head down on her shoulder.

'The sun has gone down. I was watching it while you were asleep.'

'Thinking and watching. What were you thinking?'

'I wasn't thinking.'

'You were growing up. And the sun hasn't gone down. It's just gone behind the trees. It's an old trick it has in this house, I remember.'

Caroline was not really listening. For the first time in her life she was discovering the necessity of making sounds as a means of communication. But in some secret corner of her body she was afterwards to remember what he had said about the sun going down behind the trees; and how he remembered it.

'I'm thirsty.'

Without a sound he uncoiled himself from her embrace and slid from the bed. A pale shadow crossed the room, filled a glass from the washbasin, and came silently back to her side. He sipped the glass and handed it to her. She drank it greedily, almost to the end, when she stopped herself, and held it up to him. He drained it, and set the glass down on the table beside the bed.

'The first time we drank from the same glass,' she said, drawing him down on to the bed again. But he sat on the edge and leaned his arm across her body.

'Was it?' His voice was remote and abstracted.

'Yes. And when you were sleeping a shaft of sun came in through the curtains and went through the mirror. I watched it.'

'Did you? Did it crack the mirror?'

'You'll get cold.'

'No, no.'

'Do you remember the first time we came here how we found all those withered rose-petals in the drawing-room, and how you came upstairs and left me, and I found you standing by the window?'

He turned his head and looked at the curtained window. The light from behind the curtains, spreading a diffused glow about the room, darkened his fair hair, and smudged his clear-cut profile so that it seemed to waver, appearing and dissolving, like a face glimpsed in a fog.

'Remembering already? They say that's the beginning of the end.'

'What were you remembering by that window?' she asked with a sudden flash of intuition, inspired by the irritation a woman feels when her lover reads not her thoughts, but the emotions of her body.

'I was remembering when I was young.'

'Is that why you come back here?'

'To recover my youth?' Philip chuckled.

'"To remember.'

'You're the one who's remembering.'

'No, I'm not.'

But already the irritation was dying, and she felt the need for reassurance; the reassurance a woman can only obtain by angering her lover.

'Draw back the curtains,' she said lazily.

'No.' His response was swift.

She made to get off the bed, but he caught her roughly by the arm and held her fast. For a few minutes she struggled, until languor overcame her, and she crumpled up and allowed herself to be cradled in his arms.

'You'll get cold,' she said in a muffled voice, plucking at the sheet, and attempting to draw it about his shoulders. He pulled it loose and threw it over both of them, raising her gently and making her sit by his side on the edge of the bed. Covered by the light sheet coldness suddenly overcame them, and they sat huddled together to warm each other's body. And now she craved tenderness; the gentle touching of hands, the brushing of lips, the smoothing of hair: the aftermath of passion, by which a woman seeks to reassure herself of the presence of a lover from whom she is, even in the mindless depths of pleasure, inexorably cut off. Quietly, with the dumb despair of a child who has lost a toy she knows she will never find again, Caroline began to cry.

'Such a long journey in such a short time,' said Philip softly, as he felt her tears moisten his shoulder and then trickle down his bare chest.

'I don't know why I'm crying.'

'Does anybody ever, really.'

'I never thought I'd cry with you. Sometimes when I thought I might lose you—but no, I never cried. I always laughed when I thought of you. Sometimes in the office in the middle of a letter I used to laugh for joy, and they all thought I was mad. Why am I crying?'

'Perhaps for yourself. We rarely cry for any other reason.'

'But I'm happy, Philip. I love you. Only—' She stopped and rubbed her eyes with a corner of the sheet.

'Only what?'

'I wish we hadn't come to this house.' Her voice was muffled in the linen.

'Why?' his voice was sharp.

'I don't know. It makes me afraid. There's nothing of me here.'

'Ah.'

'Sometimes when we come here and you leave me alone even for a moment I feel as though I were being watched. Like as if the place were haunted.'

He pulled the sheet from his shoulder and stood up.

'Ghosts are very fleshly things, Caroline. You have grown up too quickly.'

'I don't want to come here any more.' She drew the sheet about her tightly and shivered. Philip began to dress.

'There isn't anywhere else for us to go. Another little while and there'll be something of you here too.'

She watched him as he dressed, and felt again the over-powering sense of solitude that she had first known as she watched him sleeping by her side. When he had finished he left the room as he always did. She had once told him that she did not like him to watch her dressing. Now she regretted it. She threw on her clothes hurriedly, terrified of the darkened room, the secret all-seeing mirror, and presence of something sensed and unheard. When she finished dressing she ran to the window and drew the curtains back with a jerk that set the runners quivering like wires. The rosy light of the summer evening stained with the dark green of the trees flooded the room, and blinded her for a few seconds. Then the blue mountain cones across the bay appeared out of the darkness, and slipped into place beyond the window-panes. In a laburnum tree just below the window a thrush was singing. Caroline pressed her nose against the glass like a child at a sweet-shop, and cradled her eyes with her hands. Something moved on the lawn below. Philip walked down from the terrace and stood on the grass with his back to the house, looking out over the yellow-green sea. The thrush stopped singing and fluttered into the air. Caroline stood looking down at the small still figure on the lawn for what seemed to her a long time. Neither of them moved. Suddenly he turned round, looked up at the window, and held out his hands in a curious supplicating gesture. She started back and ran from the room, down the stairs, through the drawing-room and out on to the terrace where she stopped dead, breathing through her mouth, fighting to hold back the desire to laugh with joy. She blinked, panting and awkward, plucking at her cheap cotton frock, and rubbing the heel of one of her shoes against the worn flags of the terrace. They were still warm with the heat of the day.

Then the small fair head tilted up, the hands were held out in a beckoning gesture, and she was running down the steps into his arms.

10

SUNDAY. Along Vico Road the cars were parked bumper to bumper. Mr Quill sat in the front of the old Ford, his hat on the back of his head, reading the *Sunday Press*. Sybil dozed beside him over her copy of the *Sunday Express*. Caroline, her *Sunday Independent* unopened on her lap, was leaning forward with her chin on her clasped hands, staring out at the great bay sparkling like heated glass under the sun. Beyond the glittering thread of shingle the blue-green valley between Killiney and the mountains shimmered under the heat-haze like a lake under a morning mist. Valley and ocean rested side by side, spent and exhausted by the warmth, separated by the motionless dyke of pebbled beach. And overhead the sky was as white and freshly ironed as an airing sheet on a bush.

Mr Quill yawned.

'Nothing in the papers.'

All the windows of the car were closed, and inside it was as hot as a pot-oven at noon. It would not have occurred to any of them to let the air in. That had never been done.

'Miss Blake gets the *Sunday Times*,' said Sybil.

'I suppose I ought to go for a walk.' Mr Quill looked at his watch. Two hours to opening time.

'Mrs Abberton lives just around the corner near Killiney village. She invited me to walk in her garden, but somehow I never got round to it, and I wouldn't like to call on a Sunday, seeing that she's a Protestant.'

'Are you doing the crossword, Carry?' said her father.

57

'No, Daddy.' Caroline looked down at her paper—the President kneeling to kiss a bishop's ring on the front page —and slowly, very softly began to tear it into long thin strips.

'Everybody is out today,' said Sybil. 'Did you ever see anything like the way men are dressing now. All them colours.'

'I must do the crossword sometime,' said Mr Quill.

Caroline continued her silent work of destruction. Her father would never do the crossword.

'There's not the same class of people coming out here now as used to in the old days. Teddy-boys, if you ask me. Miss Blake was saying the same about Dun Laoghaire the other evening.'

'Very warm today. Best summer I remember for a long time. I must go for a swim.'

'I don't suppose Mrs Abberton walks along this road at all, with her lovely garden. All them glorious rhododendrons, and a private view of the bay all to herself. It's well to be some people. Caroline, are there rashers in it for the tea?'

'No, Mammy, it's too hot for rashers. You said you'd get lettuce.'

'Oh, Lord, I forgot it. Anyway I'm not hungry. Tea and brack will do us. It's too hot for anything.'

'I'm roasted.' Mr Quill leaned his head against the closed window with a sigh.

'That's very like a girl I used to know long ago. That one there with the yellow frock. Only she wouldn't be as young as that, I suppose.'

'This would be a right day for a swim in the Forty Foot.'

'Very warm today,' said Sybil. 'Best summer I remember for a long time. We used to have good summers when I was a girl.'

They relapsed into drowsy silence, staring with heavy eyes at the strolling crowd on the path. Yellow and pink and blue and red and green dresses; and fawn and black and white trousers; and multi-coloured cardigans. Eyes bright and sparkling with brine, or faded and sleepy from too much sun. Brown arms, legs and cheeks; a ripple of laughter breaking through the lazy hum of muffled voices. This was the Sunday promenade on Vico Road overlooking Killiney Bay, where the Quills went every week during the summer, hail, rain or snow, for two hours to read the newspapers, doze and watch the strollers. So set had the habit become of recent years that they went also from early spring to late autumn. And it was here one bright April day that Philip O'Connor first met Caroline; inquired of her father what she was doing; and a few days later 'phoned her at the auctioneer's office where she worked. A casual encounter between old friends against a background of such serene and luminous beauty that the cheap summer frocks, the bright pullovers, the young commonplace faces of the passers-by seemed to reflect something of its colour and grandeur, almost as if they belonged to another age, and sauntered under parasols of peacock blue.

Caroline, who had been first brought here when she was a little girl, had always enjoyed it in a mild sort of way; but now that this slumbering sea belonged to the evenings she spent with Philip, she found the excursions almost intolerable.

'Hotter and hotter,' said her father. 'Warmest summer I remember for a long time. Right weather for a swim.'

'I see in the paper here that they have snow in Spain,' said Sybil. 'Now doesn't that beat out.'

'Did I tell you that Paul has a niece home from England?'

'Did you tell me what, John?'

'I said Paul had a niece home from England.'

'Well imagine that. Miss Blake is expecting a nephew home from Kenya in September. Do you know I don't think you can believe half of what you read in these papers.'

'This is his sister's girl. Won a whole lot of money in the pools and came home for a holiday.'

'We must do the pools sometimes. Miss Blake's nephew has a lot of money of his own. Real rich he is, but he's selling his place in Kenya because of the blacks she says, and he's going to buy a house in this country.'

'Not a bit like Paul. I suppose she takes after her father.'

'Miss Blake has a whole lot of photographs of her nephew. He's not like her either. Lord, will you look at that one, the one with the red trousers. Now isn't that a disgrace. Wouldn't you be surprised that the priests would allow them to carry on like that. I don't know what the country is coming to.'

But Mr Quill was not listening. His head had fallen forward, and his chin was cosily cushioned in his white Sunday shirt.

'Carry,' said her mother in a low voice, 'do you want the *Express*? Is there anything in the *Independent*?'

But Caroline was not listening to her. A few seconds before, in a break in the crowd, she had seen Philip standing on the path looking at her.

'Carry I said—'

'I think I see Mr O'Connor.' Caroline's voice was low and casual. After the first painfully happy shock of seeing him so unexpectedly, she found herself calm and completely in control. She had noticed recently that at the slightest approach of danger, when she called Philip by his Christian name before her parents, or made a slip about the time she was supposed to be at the tennis-club, an ice calm seemed to descend upon her. It did not desert her now.

'Philip,' exclaimed Sybil, nudging her dozing husband with her elbow. 'Where is he? John, wake up.'

The crowd closed in again, but not before Caroline had seen Philip turn away and look back at somebody.

'Is his wife with him?' said Sybil. 'Oh, what way am I at all. Carry, have you a comb?'

The crowd parted again and Philip came towards them with Lilian by his side, the two little griffons trotting in front of her on green leads. Mr Quill got out of the car with some difficulty and hurried round to shake hands with his old friend. They all shook hands. They spoke of the weather. They looked at the view. They passed some comments on the other strollers. And at last, Sybil and Caroline having joined the others on the path, they sat down on the low wall with their backs to the bay and fell silent.

Lilian in her polite English way was the first to break the silence.

'We come up here occasionally on Sundays. One never tires of the view.'

'Yes, isn't it gorgeous,' said Sybil enthusiastically, staring at the road in front, on which the tar had bubbled up with the heat. 'We come up here every Sunday, don't we John?'

'Sometimes even in winter too. There's no place like it.'

'I'm sick of it,' said Caroline.

'A friend of mine lives just around the corner, a Mrs Abberton.' Sybil had been preparing her remark for some moments and did not hear what her daughter said. 'Do you know her?'

'Yes, I know her,' said Lilian, with a quick look at the young girl, who was staring in front of her with a set face. 'She lives quite near an uncle of mine. That's one of the reasons we come up here on Sundays. My uncle is away and Philip has the key.'

Caroline stood up and folded her arms across her breast. Watching the angry profile with its lower lip pushed out scornfully, Lilian wondered what had made the girl change so much since she had first met her. Perhaps, thought Lilian lazily, her back warmed by the sun, she's in love or something, and it must be boring for her to be with old people like us.

'Where is your uncle gone?' said Caroline rudely, without turning round.

'America. His two sons are there.'

'It must be wonderful to be able to get away just like that. I think your dogs are lovely.'

'They're awful rogues, aren't they?' Lilian leaned forward and fondled one of the little whiskered heads. The other dog immediately turned his back. Over his wife's bent head Caroline shot an anguished look at Philip, a look so naked and imploring that if it had been intercepted by anybody except her parents it would have completely betrayed her. Philip stooped and picked up the dog which had turned its back. Lilian sat back and smiled.

'Tubby is jealous,' she said with her deep ribald chuckle. 'Give him to me, Philip. Muff doesn't mind.'

'Extraordinary little dogs,' said Sybil. 'I was telling Miss Blake about them. Do you know Miss Blake?'

'Yes, indeed.' Lilian chuckled again and kissed the dog's head.

Is it possible, thought Caroline, that people spend their lives talking like this, or have I never heard them before? Is this the way I talk? Is this the way I sound to other people? Is Mammy really interested in whether Mrs O'Connor knows Miss Blake or not? What are they all talking about?

'How is the office, Caroline?' said Philip quietly.

It was as if he had reached out and touched her hand, soothing her in a moment of fright. She sat down again on the low wall and smiled at him in grateful misery. This was their road, their view, their country: to share it with others was hideous.

'Much the same. One of the girls got married last week.'

'Which one, Carry?' said Sybil. 'You never told me.'

'Oh, she was old. Nearly forty.'

'Gracious,' said Lilian, pulling her little dog's ear.

'We all got up a subscription and gave her a present.'

'What present did you give her, Caroline?' He came and sat down beside her, picking up Muff as he passed the others.

'A tea-service.'

'She likes you,' said Lilian to Caroline as the little dog in Philip's arms stretched its neck and licked the girl's bare arm.

'Imagine, she was nearly twenty years in the office.'

'Longer than you're alive,' said Philip.

'I never thought of that, the poor thing. Oh, isn't he nice!'

'It's a she,' said Philip.

Lilian, playing with Tubby, listened to Mrs Quill's chatter, looking at the passing crowd with a lazy indulgent eye, sensed rather than saw the young girl relaxing by her side. It was easy to keep Sybil engaged, one merely had to nod agreement with her from time to time; while her husband, his broad back hunched in the sun, seemed content merely to be with them. What an odd childlike man he is, she thought; and what a strange intense daughter they have. During a lull in Sybil's conversation she glanced round at Caroline.

'I never read the Sunday papers,' the girl was saying. 'Which ones do you get?'

'The *Times, Observer, Independent.*'

'There's never anything in any of them,' said Caroline firmly, as if she meant it.

'Well, sometimes. I rather enjoy them. I like the book-pages.'

'Do you? Do you really? Do you ever do the crossword in the *Independent*?'

How strange, thought Lilian, as she listened to this banal scrap of conversation; and she seemed so bored with what we were saying a few minutes ago. Suddenly Caroline half-turned her face towards her. She was laughing and her eyes were shining.

'Did you hear that, Daddy? Mr O'Connor says he never does the crossword either. Isn't that extraordinary!'

Lilian slumped back on the wall and held the little dog closer to her breast. She felt a little of what Caroline had felt a few minutes before; as if the idle summer chatter had no meaning, and she had been left a long way behind. But of course it had meaning for Philip and the young girl. So that's who it is, she thought, as she bent and kissed Tubby's bristly head again. And with the sudden illumination came an intense sympathy, almost a tenderness for the girl. Would she ever realize, even if I dared to tell her, that I'm only jealous of her youth, and of nothing else? It was with the greatest difficulty that she restrained herself from stroking Caroline's bare brown arm, and touching her gleaming hair. But Sybil was off again.

'Yes, Mrs Quill, I do like rhododendrons.'

'We're going to put some at the bottom of our garden, aren't we, John?'

'Mnn?'

'I said—'

'I love those little dogs,' said Caroline to Philip. They suddenly seemed to be of intense interest since Muff had climbed off Philip's knee and come to sit on hers.

'They're quaint little things,' said Philip.

'Yes, that's the word, that's just what they are. Quaint.'

'Of course they don't much mind about me. They're very much one-man dogs, and they worship Lilian.'

'I love dogs,' said Caroline passionately. 'Don't you?'

'Not much, I'm afraid. I don't get on very well with animals.'

'Don't you? I don't believe that.'

'It's true.'

The empty, idle chatter flowed back and forth full of meaning and significance for Caroline. Mr Quill looked at his watch and frowned. I wish to God, he thought, they'd stop chattering. I never heard such nonsense, and Mick's will be open in an hour.

11

'LOVE,' said Mr Quill with a secret smile, 'is a queer thing.'

'Not unless you're queer,' said Miss Lee brightly.

'What day is it today?' said Paul.

'Why, Wednesday, Uncle Paul. Are you feeling all right? Would you like to go home and lie down?'

'People don't understand about love,' went on Mr Quill doggedly. 'That's what's wrong with them.'

'I do. I know all about love. I'll tell you about it any time you like.'

Mr Quill paused and dragged his gaze away from the far horizon over the top of Mick's counter and looked at Miss Lee pityingly.

'Is that so?'

'What do you mean is that so? It certainly is so.'

'Wednesday did you say?' Wednesday was Paul's free day. No collections. No raffles. It was his night for getting really drunk. He folded his hands across his stomach and allowed his head to rest on his chest. A babyish trickle of saliva trickled from the corner of his mouth. His pimple was on the wane.

'Nothing ever happens on Wednesday,' he murmured, wiping his mouth with the crook of his elbow. 'Thank God.'

'Well, what do you mean?' said Miss Lee to Mr Quill.

'Aw, what would you know about it. Sure you aren't even married.'

Iris's mouth dropped open; but she managed to pull herself together with a little twist of the shoulders. Then she stood up and patted her shining hair.

'My round.'

'I don't like this business of women buying rounds,' said Mr Quill after she had gone to the counter. He unbuttoned his jacket, and settled his shirt tidily inside his trousers. Outside the sun shone low in the orange sky; inside, where the denizens of Mick's crouched over their pints, fearful of the insidious fresh air, it was smelly and thick-aired as a prehistoric cave in which people huddled together for fear of the wild animals outside.

Paul, who never quite dropped off to sleep, because of his habit of carrying large sums of gambling contributions, opened one eye.

'Give the woman her head. Hasn't she got the vote ?'

'I don't like it. I don't care what you say. I never let a woman buy a drink for me in my life. What I always say is—'

He was unable to say what he thought, for at that moment Miss Lee arrived back at the table, with flushed face and tearful eyes, and announced in a loud voice for all the bar to hear, that she had been insulted, and that if either of them was half a man he would knock down the insolent pup who had spoken to a lady in such terms. Then she sank into her chair, covered her eyes with her hands, and a tiny trickle of black-stained tears rolled down her cheeks.

Paul opened both eyes and regarded his niece with eyes as cold and hard as pebbles.

'Why,' he inquired with mild interest, 'didn't you spit in his eye ?'

'Nobody has ever spoken to me like that in the whole course of my life,' sobbed Iris. 'I'll never be able to hold my head up again as long as I live. Never.'

'Yes, you will,' said Paul. 'When you wash your face.'

Suddenly she thumped the table with her tiny fists and glared at Mr Quill.

'Are you a man or aren't you ?' she screamed. 'Are you going to sit there like an ox and let a lady friend be insulted like that ?' She twisted round and pointed a scarlet-nailed finger at the only man in the bar who had not turned towards them. Faces with eager, malicious eyes pointed in their direction; talk dribbled and ceased like a drying tap;

the old barman stood frozen as in a photograph, with a tray of pints held against his chest.

'Wednesday,' sighed Paul sadly, 'the quietest night in the week.'

'Well, do something,' insisted Miss Lee hysterically.

Mr Quill cleared his throat, buttoned his jacket and rose slowly to his feet. The bar leaned forward on its toes; the barman's tray tilted sideways, a little out of focus; somebody in the back giggled nervously.

'Where is he?' said Mr Quill mildly.

'There, there.' Miss Lee stood up and pointed at the back, which to Mr Quill seemed propped up against the counter like a sack of potatoes. He squared his broad shoulders and ambled over. He tapped the man's arm gently with his forefinger. It was the same man he had been talking to on the evening of Paul's absence, when Miss Lee had made her first appearance in the bar.

'Hullo, there,' said the man amiably.

'Would you mind stepping out to the back for a few minutes?' said Mr Quill sternly.

'Sure. Wait till I finish my pint.'

'Now, now, gentlemen,' said the barman.

Somebody hiccoughed loudly. Miss Lee continued to sniff.

'Lovely weather for this time of year,' said a voice at the back of the bar in an artificial tone. Nobody responded. The man finished his pint and followed Mr Quill through the ranks that parted like the Red Sea to let them pass. Silence enclosed them, like frozen waves, until they had stepped out of the back door into the concrete yard behind. Then there was a rush for the window overlooking it, and talk bubbled up again like a wilderness of uncapped soda bottles.

'It's going to be a massacre. The little fellow will be destroyed.'

'Where are they going I can't see? Are they making for the jacks?'

'Where else? That's where they always go.'

'Oh, God, there's many a man went in there was never seen again.'

'Flushed down the drain. Do you remember the Canadian that was three days dead in there before they found him?'

'I wouldn't mind a Canadian. This is going to be a real fight. Besides he died of a stroke.'

'In the middle of all this ridiculous pother I'm left with an empty glass,' said Paul. 'And on Wednesday too. I was better off when I bought my own drink. Are you going to stand your round or aren't you?'

'Oh, Uncle Paul, do you think anything will happen to him? Suppose the other fellow has a knife on him.'

'I can see that you're not.' Paul got up and carried his own glass to the counter.

Outside Mr Quill and the red-haired man proceeded on their way towards the iron-roofed, white-washed enclosure which served as a lavatory for the public bar. They were well aware of the eyes fixed on their backs as they walked calmly in single file, Mr Quill leading the way, towards their destination. At the door Mr Quill stepped back and allowed his adversary the privilege of entering first. Inside they were assailed by the usual smells; and Mr Quill, who had never been in the public bar in his life and was unfamiliar with its amenities, was at a loss for some moments in the murky gloom.

'Wait till I have a pump,' said the red-haired man.

'I'll join you.'

They stood shoulder to shoulder before the trickling wall. Mr Quill, staring dreamily in front of him, became aware, as his eyes grew accustomed to the half-light, of some intricate and curiously detailed drawings on the wall. He studied these *graffiti* with some interest for a few moments, and then recoiled, having finished his business in quicker time than his enemy.

'Isn't it horrible the things that are written up here,'

he said in a shocked voice. 'You wouldn't see the like of that in the saloon toilet.'

'Were you ever in the Green Bar down the road?' said the man, studying the wall with deep interest.

'No.'

'Well you should go. There's nothing like it in the whole of Dublin. I brought an American there once and he took it all down in a notebook. Said he never saw the like of it in his life. Boy, it's great! This is only muck compared with it. No imagination.'

'Muck is right.'

'Not in the same class at all as the Green Bar. Even the men who go into the public bar at Mick's are kind of refined. This stuff here shows no acquaintance at all with the true facts of life.'

'I'll say it doesn't. Life is beautiful.'

'What's that you said?' The man was still comfortably relieving himself, and continuing his study of the *graffiti*.

'I said life is beautiful.' He waved one hand in the direction of the wall, holding the other in front of his nose to filter the smell. 'Not like that.'

'That's right. This is only third-rate stuff. But you should go to the Green Bar. You'd enjoy that. That's really beautiful. Beautiful. It'd rise a bishop.'

'When you think of all the good things in life, and the men that died to make this country free, it's shocking to see stuff like that,' said Mr Quill, who was becoming affected by the smell of the place. 'Stinking, that's what it is.'

'I can see that you're a connoisseur. That's why I say you ought to go to the Green Bar. This is only amateur stuff.'

'Are you all right?' said Mr Quill anxiously. The red-haired man seemed to have a remarkable capacity, and was still placidly going about his business.

'I have a terrible time with my kidneys. And it isn't only

69

that. It's the size of it, I'm that big. The bigger you are the longer it takes you.'

But at length he buttoned his trousers, and turned round, patting himself affectionately. Then he produced a packet of cigarettes, which he offered to Mr Quill. Now neither of them had the slightest intention of dishonouring the men of Ireland by fighting over a woman. Face however had to be saved. Mr Quill felt that it would not be quite the thing to smoke with a man he was supposed to be battering against the walls of the urinal. The red-haired man lit up and peered gloomily again at the *graffiti*.

'You're quite right,' he said. 'They're no good. Kid stuff. The fellow that did that one there in the corner doesn't know what he has it for. I'd show him.'

'Now about this matter we're supposed to be discussing,' said Mr Quill ponderously.

'My name is Murphy. Jack Murphy. My friends call me Crowbar Jack. There's a poem about it up in the Green Bar. That's something, I can tell you.'

'Pleased to meet you. The name is Quill, John Quill.'

'Oh I know your name. Women are awful aren't they? There's no accounting for them.'

'There are,' said Mr Quill firmly, 'women and women. Some are ladies. What did you say to her anyway?'

'Well it was like this. She came up to the bar and nearly upset a pint all over my new shirt, forty-two-and-sixpence in Cleary's out of my overtime money. I worked for this shirt I can tell you, wore myself to the bone. So she said to me, and mind you I was minding my own business after coming from confession and all, and said "why don't you keep your elbows to yourself?", so I told her that if I was holding my pint at an angle it was my own pint and I worked hard for it, and I wasn't in Mick's looking for women to pick me up and buy me drinks. That's what I said to her. So then she started screaming the place down. You'd imagine I took it out and waved it in front of her. Pity I didn't. That might quieten her down.'

'She's buying no drinks for me,' said Mr Quill with some heat. 'I told her that flat. But she wants to treat her uncle. She won't even let him buy the bottle of whiskey that was his habit every night. She picked up all this in England.'

'I can see that. England has the women of Ireland destroyed. Are you sure you won't have a cigarette?'

'No, thanks. All the same I think you ought to apologize to the lady. After all a lady is a lady.'

'You wouldn't want her to buy you a drink, now would you, I mean to say.'

'I certainly would not. I told her that fifty times if I told her once. All the same she's with me, I mean she's with Paul, and I can't let Paul down.'

'God no,' said Murphy warmly, 'you can not. Everything was grand for the two of you until she came.' He spat into the urinal. 'England, that's what it is. Half the women have to pay for it over there when they want it. Sure they're not men at all. I knew you weren't taking drinks from her.'

'Maybe,' said Mr Quill, who was now beginning to be overcome by the murk of the place, and whose head was reeling, 'if you bought her a drink or something just to show that there's no hard feelings.'

'Oh, I don't mind that.' Murphy tapped ash on to the slimy floor. 'But at a later date. I'm fed up with this place anyhow. I think I'll go to the Green Bar.'

Mr Quill groped his way towards the door in search of fresh air.

'If you come back into Mick's you'll have to buy her a drink, won't you? All she wants is an apology. You know what women are.'

'Don't I but. Will she be here long do you think?'

'She says she's home for a month or two.'

'Jesus.'

'If I were you I'd go out the back wicket and go up to the Green Bar. I'll tip you off when she's out of the country.'

Honour was satisfied. Murphy would not have to undergo the indignity of apologizing to a lady: Mr Quill would be left in possession of the field.

'I'll stay in here for a bit. My kidneys are killing me. Besides I want to touch up some of the poems in here. They're not fit for any self-respecting man to read. I have a great one called *The Shape of Things to Come*. Did you ever hear it? Well it's up in the Green Bar. Why don't you come in there some night and have a jar? I never saw a woman in the Green Bar in my life.'

'Thanks, I will.' Mr Quill reeled out into the yard, and the watchers behind the window concluded that it must have been a fierce encounter when they saw the big man steadying himself against the wall, and wiping his clammy forehead with his sleeve.

'Holy God,' said one of them in an admiring voice, 'the other fellow must be in little bits.'

Their admiration was increased when Mr Quill made his reappearance; pale, a little green at the gills, but clearly unscratched. He walked through the bar in a religious silence, his strong well-moulded chin thrust forward. Miss Lee jumped to her feet when she saw him approach, and threw her arms about his neck.

'Oh, John, John,' she cried, 'Johnny darling.'

Mr. Quill, who was too sick to realize the sensation this exhibition made on the denizens of Mick's, or the various constructions that would be put upon it, disengaged himself, not without dignity, and sank into his chair.

'Home is the hero,' said Paul. 'For God's sake.'

'And now darlings,' said Miss Lee, throwing out her arms in a grand theatrical gesture, 'the drinks are on me.'

12

THROUGH the open french window came an over-powering scent of roses: climbing roses on the walls of the house, pot roses on the terrace, standard roses lined along the path below, and beyond, bed after bed of lustrous blobs of colour.

'Are you sure you won't catch cold with the window open?' said Lilian, who would have welcomed the opportunity of shutting out the heavy cloying smell.

'If you don't like the scent of my roses why don't you say so, dear?' said Miss Blake in the kindly voice she used for delivering a particularly barbed remark. 'You used to be so refreshingly honest when you came here. Now you're getting worse than the Irish. But do close the window if you want to.'

Lilian remained seated. One always ended up by doing none of the things one wanted to do with Miss Blake.

The old lady was sitting up in the big carved mahogany bed she had put in the drawing-room to spare herself the stairs. A dressing-table had taken the place of a love-seat under a foggy painting of Highland cattle between two of the windows; and a huge wardrobe had been placed alongside a bookcase in which reposed, tier upon tier, the works of the Victorian novelists in dusty, leather-bound splendour. Every piece of furniture in the shabby room was of mahogany; every chair and sofa was quilted, and on the mantelpiece, among the china dogs and the glass-domed wax flowers, a tinted photograph of Queen Victoria was enshrined in bulging, blue-eyed majesty.

Miss Blake was smoking one of Lilian's cigarettes, holding it between her thumb and forefinger with their black-edged nails, and inhaling it with short noisy sucks. She had been regaling Lilian with some scurrilous gossip about a royal couple from a Bavarian principality who had recently been fêted in Dublin because the Princess, an Irish-

American, had come to visit her grandfather's cabin in Tipperary.

'Well, dear,' she went on, 'as I was saying, she's been having some very bad publicity in America, which is why they fixed up this visit, so of course she was on her best behaviour. The current lover, a Munich policeman. was left behind. Prince Charming however is a different kettle of fish. He can't be kept from the boys, and since he was bored to tears, there were incidents that would have blown the roofs off any other town except Dublin, where it's not supposed to exist. Sodom, dear, and begorrah, as they say. Of course she took good care to bring the children—both fathered by the policeman naturally—and that clinched the deal.'

Miss Blake broke off her recital and gurgled with amusement: a deep, throaty chuckle, which Lilian had over the years managed to pick up. People rarely escaped from Miss Blake's powerful personality without some sign of their association with her: a gesture, an inflexion of speech, a fondness for the hideous Victorian furniture which filled her house, or the heavy Victorian novels which she pretended to read. Many there were who determined to grow roses in gardens less suitable than the half-acre in which they first saw them blooming in rich profusion.

Lilian herself had noticed many of those little mannerisms among the old woman's circle; quite unaware that she also was marked with the sign. But a certain unassailable honesty of mind had preserved her from the less attractive aspects of Rose Blake's influence. Lacking the self-devouring nature, the essential barrenness of soul in which gossip flourishes, much of the spite that Rose wove about her like a poisoned web escaped Lilian completely. Having a somewhat unimaginative mind she listened to the stream of ill-natured stories without any of the ghoulish glee which their scabrous details inspired in others: indeed most of them bored her. Rose was well aware of this; and finding her salacious morsels received with polite indifference was

74

apt to aim her barbs at Lilian herself. This morning, cosy in bed, with a packet of cigarettes she had no intention of returning, she was saving a particularly sharp one against the moment her visitor's attention wandered.

'You look tired, dear,' she said gently. 'What is it? Philip?'

Lilian shrugged.

'You're not having enough fun, dear. You and Philip don't go out nearly enough together. You know how Edwardian Dublin is—you've got to present a face to the public. As it is people are beginning to talk.'

'You mean about Philip and the little Quill girl?' Lilian jerked up her head with one of her awkwardly direct movements, and confronted the old woman. Miss Blake blinked, and cleared her throat so loudly and at such length that Lilian started and looked at the old-fashioned jar of smelling salts on the dressing-table.

'I'm perfectly all right, dear,' said Rose in a hard clear voice. She was very annoyed with the younger woman for anticipating her. Lilian, who always thought of Miss Blake as monstrously formidable, did not realize that her own straightforward candour was a source of constant embarrassment in a society where nothing was ever stated directly. 'I had no idea you knew, and were so complacent. It was Dolly Abberton told me. Apparently he meets her at your Uncle Jim's house. When I heard that I made up my mind to tell you. That really shocked me.'

'But you told me about all the others too, didn't you?' said Lilian calmly. 'You know perfectly well that Philip's been having these little affairs for years. They don't really mean anything to him at all.'

'I know that,' said Miss Blake impatiently. 'But this is different. Your Uncle Jim is one of my oldest friends. It's shocking of Philip to bring one of his little pieces into the house where he met you, and proposed to you. It looks as though he doesn't care what people say any more.'

'For heaven's sake, don't be such a hypocrite, Rose,'

75

snapped Lilian, angered at last now that the old woman had hit upon the one aspect of the affair that really wounded her. 'You don't give a hoot where he brings her, any more than you give a hoot about Philip, or about this unfortunate child who's in love with him.'

'Well, really, Lilian—'

'I've seen them together. She's not just another "little piece" as you put it. She's young and rather beautiful, and very much in love, and she's going to get very hurt. I've got used to Philip's little affairs, or at least I've learned to put up with them, for the simple reason that I love him.'

Miss Blake shifted uncomfortably and lit another cigarette. This aspect of Lilian—her complete refusal to conceal anything that she felt strongly about—always disconcerted her. Rose Blake's whole life, like that of so many of her compatriots, had been an elaborate masked ball to which she had gained admittance without paying the subscription. Sincerity struck her as something obscene, in a way that obscenity itself never did.

'Jasus,' she said, falling into the Dublin slang she adopted whenever she was embarrassed,' will ya listen ta tha'! A wummum in holy bedlock takin' the part of her husban's liddle mot. Mother a God!'

'How long have you known?' said Lilian with a frown.

'Oh, for some weeks,' lied Rose glibly. She had heard the news the night before. 'Dolly's bedroom looks straight on to your Uncle Jim's gate, and you know what an old curtain-twitcher she is. And anyway you can't really get away with it in Dublin. It's like trying to swim naked in a public bath. Well, go on dear.'

But Lilian had caught the gleam of prurient curiosity in the old woman's eye. And although she felt badly in need of talking about Philip, and had come to Rose half-hoping that she would know, as she seemed to know about everything, she suddenly realized that she did not want to speak about it. It was not simply out of loyalty to Philip, since she did not believe that pretending that one knew nothing was the truest kind of loyalty, especially in Dublin where some-body was sure to tell her at some time or another 'for her own good'. Over the years she had come to expect that; and preferred to talk to Rose, about whom she had no illusions, and whose malice she had grown accustomed to, and no longer very much minded. The old woman had helped to prepare her for the incestuous family atmosphere of Dub-lin, with its love-hate complexes and its battery of private jokes, to which she was particularly vulnerable as an out-sider, and the wife of a man who was well known and un-faithful. This, and the stubborn loyalty that was one of her deepest instincts, had preserved her friendship with Rose, who, twenty-five years earlier in her uncle's summer garden, had with her curious oblique charm, her eight-eenth-century freedom of speech, and her earthy vitality, seemed to her to personify the very spirit of Ireland.

Rose sensed her withdrawal, with the delicate perception of a woman who has spent her life watching the effect she made on others. She shifted the conversation to a less dangerous level, which without completely shelving the subject allowed them to continue it without speaking directly of Philip.

'I know the girl's mother,' she said briskly. 'A harmless poor creature who does odd jobs for me from time to time. Met her on top of a tram where she lent me a penny for the fare. You know how hopeless I am with money. Of course I called next day to give it back to her.'

Lilian, who had gone to stand at one of the windows, could not help smiling at her own reflection in the glass, a reflection that glimmered like a ghost against the blazing beds of roses. She knew Rose's trick of borrowing small sums from new acquaintances which she was careful to pay back later, an attention which always made a deep im-pression, since she was known to be a very rich old lady. She was not so scrupulous about returning the attentions in cash and kind which she demanded later, and somehow always managed to get.

'Yes, I know them too. Mr Quill and Philip come from the same place, they used to be friends at school.'

'Well, all's fair in love and war, dear. I must say it seems a bit shocking to me, but it'll blow over. Philip will get tired of the girl, her father will get to hear of it, and that will be the end of another beautiful friendship. Not that old Quill can afford any kind of moral attitude himself. He's on the town every night with the lost awful little bar-maid type home from England.'

'Oh, no, Rose! I don't believe it.'

'Oh, yes, dear. You know I often drop into a few of the pubs in Dun Laoghaire for cigarettes for my guests. So much more interesting and amusing than the tobacconists. Well, they're in a dive called Mick's every night. The other night somebody called her a tart to her face—not far off the mark I should say—and Quill dragged him out into the yard and beat him up. There was the most awful shindy.' Rose chuckled cosily. 'Disgusting.'

Lilian did not reply. She was very tired. Beyond the burning garden with its riot of impressionistic colour, a line of gnarled chestnut trees stained the sky like a blot of a sheet of blue writing-paper. Lilian suddenly realized, with that intensity of physical perception that we experience when we are emotionally aroused, that she felt trapped, as though the trees were a wall, and the garden a poisoned place through which she could never walk. She felt her breathing grow light and shallow, and her eyebrows tickled with sweat. She turned back, her eyes flickering restlessly about the room which she thought she knew down to the last hideous inch of dark red wallpaper. But now it seemed full of the sinister detail of a place of imprisonment. She saw the grimy finger-marks on the unpolished tables; the damp stains like congealed blood on the walls; the ashen dust on the china ornaments; the frayed patches in the faded blue carpet; the crazy map of cracks on the ceiling; and the shimmering little cobwebs in the corners. And she became aware as she had never done before of the smell of the room; and realized that age, and malice and the absence of love, have a physical manifestation as sour as the odour of unwashed bodies. It wasn't simply the musty smell of an untidy room inhabited by a none too fastidious old woman—a smell which the scent of the roses emphasized rather than concealed: it was the shock of recognition that we sometimes experience on looking at a dead body, a bitter face, a mouth twisted with lust. How many times had she sat in this room listening to the same sort of talk about other people. It seemed to her that she had spent a great deal of her life in just that way: because she was bored, because it was necessary to have somebody to talk to, because one went on calling on old acquaintances. And now for the first time she realized that after so many years she could not have escaped without being tainted in some way. Must all of us, she thought, who love and who desperately want to be loved in return and somehow fail, end up like this? Did this horrible woman love somebody once? Can I go on loving for very much longer without suddenly cracking up and finding that I no longer care?

It had not seemed impossible, when she had got over the first shock of discovering that Philip no longer loved her and was constantly unfaithful, to go on finding excuses for him. It seemed in a way a development of passion into something deeper and more understanding. But now she was faced with the realization that even that kind of love, which she had clung to because it was the only kind permitted her, can come to an end. Philip's affairs had not really taken so very much away from her, because out of an instinct for self-preservation she had never allowed herself to take them too seriously. And she had the memory, which grew more vivid with the years, of an old house and garden where it had begun. Love has its symbolism. We cannot love without associating that love with something less destructible than ourselves: a book, a stretch of beach, a house. For Lilian that image had been her uncle's house, to which she had come for a fortnight's holiday in 1945; where she had met Philip; and where she had stayed for three months until their marriage. For some women the certain knowledge of having once been loved, no matter for how short a time, is enough to last them the rest of their lives. Most of Philip's affairs that Lilian had knowledge of —and Dublin made sure that she knew of all of them— were the usual exercises in physical vanity: graceful, she was sure, since he was not a coarse man, and possessed of a certain delicacy; but essentially empty. A sort of hieratic dance in which one changed partners from time to time. Most of the women had been married; wives of friends and acquaintances: none, so far as she knew, were deeply involved.

Was it because he had brought Caroline to the place she had thought of all those years as belonging to her alone that Lilian felt so hurt about this affair ? Or was it that both of them were simply growing older: the one no longer caring for appearance as he plunged deeper into the quest for pleasure; the other because she was tired and beginning to be bitter ?

As she struggled with her memories Lilian experienced a moment of panic, and realized that she was staring at Rose; and that the old woman was sitting bolt upright in the bed, staring back at her with eyes opened wide as if she had just suffered a sharp attack of pain. Lilian blinked, and began to scrabble in her handbag for her car keys. She could think of nothing to say. She only wanted to escape from the room, which suddenly seemed to her to be a hideous caricature of what the future might be.

But Rose had read with deadly accuracy that part of her thoughts which applied to herself. Incapable of accepting the fact that she no longer meant anything to anybody, she clawed her way to attention like a drowning man clinging to a collapsing bank. Laughter she could still provoke with her light malicious gossip: to play the clown is always the fate of those who have no place in the scheme of things. If you can make people laugh they are more inclined to tolerate you. And disgust, which she knew she sometimes inspired in others, was better than indifference. Yet Rose Blake had never ceased to resent it.

'It comes on so gradually, dear,' she said softly, 'that you hardly notice it. Until of course one meets somebody like you.'

13

'SOMEDAY I suppose you'll come back here, and wonder who it was you used to meet here, and what became of her.'

'Someday you'll pass the gate, and wonder who it was you used to visit here and what was his name.'

'No, I won't. I'll always remember.'

Philip and Caroline were walking arm in arm across the lawn, pursued by their own shadows that blended and came to life and then blended again with the lengthening shadows of the trees. The great crouching shade of the house had already claimed almost half of the lawn, turning the grass mole-green, and was edging inch by inch like a night tide towards the couple walking in the sun.

'You don't believe that?' said Caroline.

'We have this,' said Philip, taking her hand and slipping her fingers between his own.

'Yes, we have this. Now. But we won't always have it.'

'How can you tell that?' Philip's voice was low and he held her fingers as gently as if she were a child. 'After all I'm old enough to be your father. Someday you'll meet somebody of your own age, and then you'll forget. You'd be surprised how easy it is to forget. You'll see.'

'Easy for you too?'

'It's so very easy to grow old.'

'And do you stop loving when you grow old?'

Philip disengaged himself and stopped at the edge of the growing shadow of the house, his small head lifted high, looking away from her across the dappled garden to where a patch of ink blue sea showed through a gap in the hedge.

'No,' he said sadly, 'you go on.'

'You mean,' she insisted, frightened and slightly angry at his detachment, 'you go on loving other people.'

He was silent for a long time, while she stood waiting humbly by his side, until they both felt the chill of the gathering shade, and turned in the same instant towards each other. Philip reached out and touched her cheek with his fingertips, moving them slowly with infinite tenderness across the smooth warm skin; across her mouth, tracing the delicate moulding of her chin, and encircling her neck with his thumb and forefinger. Then with equal gentleness he took her hand and held it against his own cheek.

'I'm sorry,' he murmured, 'that I cannot make you happy.'

It was her turn to remain silent; his to feel the need to talk. He did not understand the overwhelming tenderness, the aching and solitary male protectiveness that she inspired in him. He had always been a considerate lover; even when, as in most of his affairs, he had merely sought to indulge that refined and dangerous sensuality which made him so attractive to women; especially those women who had discovered, consciously or unconsciously with their husbands, that a man without a streak of femininity in his nature is rarely a good lover.

'I don't want to hurt you, my Caroline. And you are already a little hurt, aren't you?'

She shook her head, and then laid her forehead on his shoulder to hide the tears that had started to her eyes. She wept silently, without shivering, like a child who wakes in the dark and is afraid to disturb the ghost that lurks in the corner of the room.

'You mustn't be hurt, you shouldn't be. Growing up shouldn't be like this. You should never have met me. I should never have seen you again. I should have counted the years. But they pass so quickly that you cease to count them, until someday you do something, or meet somebody like you, and you think you're like them, and then you suddenly realize that you're not.'

The shadow of the house had crept silently about them as they stood on the lawn; and now they clung together in the shade: Caroline stiff and mute with grief; Philip aware for the first time that he was cold, and that he was holding the young girl not only out of tenderness, but also out of the need for warmth.

'Why, it seems only yesterday that I came here and—' he broke off, biting his lip, and staring up at the blind windows of the house. Caroline raised her forehead from his shoulder and held the back of her hand before her eyes.

'We're standing in the shade,' she said. 'Come into the sun.'

He followed her, soundless from the shadows into the bright patch of sunlight that lingered on the other side of the lawn. As they walked side by side he did not realize that the shadows that pursued him were not only those made by the dying of the sun. He did not know that events curl and twist and strike back like serpents trodden by careless feet; that things and emotions flow together like a stream over pebbles; that none of our actions is entirely free; and that in fleeing from something we dread we are apt to entangle ourselves in something equally terrible, but of a similar nature, because we go on responding to those passions of love, avarice, pride and hope that have made us what we are. If Philip O'Connor had used his young mistress in a deliberate attempt to recapture the past; to find in her a reflection of the young girl he had loved and married, he would have created a pleasant summer idyll; a graceful comedy in which he only half-believed. A clear-sighted man, he would have tempered the game with irony.

It should have been very much like his other affairs; and Caroline, young as she was, would have sensed that protective mockery which always prevents the young and innocent from making the final desperate commitment. But the real destroyers are always unaware of the destruction they work. Love that can be explained, analysed and understood is a plaything. We are only obsessed, saved or destroyed by the unknown. Philip did not know that the overwhelming tenderness that Caroline inspired in him was a reflection of the only passion he had ever experienced in his life: the delicate, shy, protective love he had felt for the awkward young girl he had met in that same garden so long ago. Nor did he know that he was no longer capable of such an emotion; that the years of self-sufficiency had taken their toll; and that even in his short-lived love for his wife there had been an element of possessiveness—of protecting something that he wanted to belong to him alone. When he ceased to love his wife it was because he could never possess her entirely. He was never to discover that the one thing you cannot own is somebody who really loves you.

Irony is all of the surface; self-deception is not. There had been enough of tenderness in Philip's love-making to make Caroline believe in it, since on a certain level he believed in it himself. When she was unhappy she did not realize that in some secret corner of her heart she sensed, as every woman does in an unhappy love-affair, that she had been betrayed—a woman, unlike a man, never loves with the eye alone. And then there were so many reasons why she should have been sometimes unhappy: she could never show Philip proudly in public as her lover; they could not meet often, and then only for a short time; she could never marry him. And when she sometimes wept Philip thought of the same things. It made him even more gentle with her; unaware that deception feeds upon deception.

'Let's walk in the sun,' he said now, taking her arm

again, and making for the patch of sunlight that every moment grew smaller as the shadow of the trees reached out towards the shade of the house like two hands stretching across a sunny stream.

'Come into the house,' he said after a long silence.

'No.'

'Why?'

'I'm afraid of that house. I think it's haunted. It's full of shadows.'

'It's full of shadows out here too. Come.'

He touched her face again with his small delicate hands, soothing her as one would a small frightened child. As the shadows crept across the small patch of sunlit lawn, and the birds quietened in the darkening trees, it seemed to Philip that he had never felt such an aching sense of protectiveness for anyone as he did for the troubled young girl who followed him silently into the house.

And tenderness there was in his love-making in the dim room at the window of which a few weeks ago she had stood looking down at his beckoning figure on the lawn. But it was the gentleness of an experienced sensuality. The lips which sought to silence Caroline's fears were tentative only with the deliberate rejection of a present pleasure; the slight supple body which pressed itself against the young girl's with such protective insistence did not seek ultimately to shield, but to explore; and the hands which undressed her with such infinite patience and care had learned their subtle mastery in long years of clandestine love-making.

But for those who so tragically cannot know themselves inanimate things hold a menace which is never apparent to the undeceived. The lurking mirror, the long wraith-like curtains seemed to Caroline as she lay, physically quietened by her lover's gentle hands, to pass dumb judgment upon her. It was not simply that she found herself in a strange and totally new atmosphere—an old, richly furnished house, redolent of generations of quietly expensive living. It was not that it was for the moment uninhabited, for lovers have always sought solitude. It was a curious feeling of being made to play a part against a background to which she would be forever a stranger.

What Caroline did not know was that she, no less than Philip, was being pursued by the past; by a love that had once been reflected in those dim mirrors, proudly admitted in that sunny garden, and watched over by the dumb guardians of an old house, to which Philip in some dark corner of his mind was bound. When, with a little cry, she turned to her lover as the last flicker of light died in the mirror, she did not know that what she was afraid of was the presence of love itself, strong, triumphant, undefeated, like the atmosphere of purity in some holy place, sanctified by the prayers of uncounted generations of the dead.

14

SUMMER unfurled across the city like a silken banner. The salt-blue sky quivered with dappled light, as if it were reflecting the shimmering beaches and the winking sea that lapped them. The mountains that guard Dublin to the south were outlined as faintly as steeples in a shallow pool. And to those who climbed them, seeking release from the boiling streets that hissed under the slow-moving traffic, it seemed that the great plain that stretched beyond the city to the horizons of the west had been touched with gold: a mirage of summer corn. Dublin hung its doors with stripped awnings and put out more shutters. The streets blossomed with flowery dresses like cherry trees. Cats slept in the shade of milk-jugs crowned with saucers and immersed in basins of cold water on tenement ledges. Old ladies sighed for parasols; and old gentlemen resurrected straw hats and wore them at a rakish angle. From the narrow lane-ways behind the great squares and the dusty Victorian streets passers-by were assailed by a peculiar smell like rotting cabbage: the miasma of human decay that festers more strongly in the sun. But the old women and the slumbering men, who sat on the steps of the blind-eyed tenements, were content to take their fill of the blond sauntering days: it was a miraculous summer.

But Mr Quill was worried. He did not get into summer clothes. Indeed he did not possess any, regarding slacks and bright jackets with an unfavourable eye. Every day he drove to work and walked to his office in his neat blue suit and shining white shirt. And every afternoon he drove home and had tea with his wife and daughter. If he noticed that Caroline had changed, was more silent, paler with dark circles under her eyes, he would have put it down to the long hot summer. But he did not notice. Nothing had ever happened in the little red-brick house with its tiny patch of unmown lawn to upset the routine of twenty years. Mr Quill got up at the same time every morning. Sybil cooked breakfast while he shaved. Caroline set the table; and they all sat down together at eight o'clock. Then he rose, stretched himself, and stood looking out dreamily on the garden, with his hands in his pockets, while the women drank their third cup of tea. Then he kissed them and ambled out to the car, beginning the day with a slow ruthless twist of the starting-handle, an operation which made Sybil deeply ashamed when she thought of all the other cars in the terrace starting effortlessly with the press of a button. Caroline helped her mother with the wash-up. She did not have to leave until twenty past nine; and then walked down the road half a mile to the office where she worked. Morning followed morning like sheep filing through a gap on a sleepless night.

Or so it would have seemed to Sybil. For Caroline nothing would ever be the same again; and Mr Quill's world had recently been altogether upset. For the past week or two he had ceased to drink in Mick's in the evenings; and had taken his custom to the Green Bar, where he was sometimes joined by the red-haired Murphy over a few pints. Although he did not very much care for his new friend, whose conversation compared very unfavourably with Paul's, they had a common bond of sympathy: for they were both exiled because of Miss Lee. Since the night when they had fought for her honour Mr Quill had not had a moment's peace. She rang him up in the office; she discovered the café where he took his luncheon with his colleagues, and installed herself beside them. She leaned over and joined in their conversation, which had been sacred for twenty-five years to women in the abstract. She waited for him outside the Department at the end of the day and begged a lift home. Mr Quill could not refuse her because of Paul. She made his life a hell.

'Who's that one?' asked his colleague of nineteen years at the next desk in the Department. 'She doesn't look like the one you were telling me about that you brought up Dalkey Hill, to look at the view I don't think.'

In his misery Mr Quill's alter ego did not desert him.

'That's another one,' he said with the little secret smile, which over the years had become automatic. 'I finished with this one a long time ago, but she won't let me alone.'

'You mean to say you don't want anything to do with that blonde dish?'

'Not any more.'

The man whistled. Mr Quill's stock at the Department went up. He bore it with his accustomed aplomb. He went about his work of checking forms with the self-conscious modesty of a miler who has just broken a world record. He could do nothing wrong. When he abandoned his seat at the café, and wandered disconsolately from one shabby restaurant to another in search of peace, his colleagues understood perfectly; he was a man fatal to women. There was danger in his slow smile; satiation in his heavy eyes;

ruthlessness in his small deliberate hands. He had come to the fulfilment of his dreams; and he was miserable. The long cosy evenings with Paul were no more: he was reduced to the garish splendour of the Green Bar, inside the door of which a hideous juke-box howled like a man-woman for its demon lover. He was an exile; and like all exiles he expected his fellow expatriates to share his disengagement.

It was therefore a very considerable shock to him to find his new friend Murphy in the Green Bar one evening sitting intimately with Miss Lee over two glasses of whiskey.

'Well, for heaven's sake if it isn't Johnny boy. Come and join the party, dear.'

'Iris and me have made it up,' said Murphy, with a none-too-friendly glance at his former friend-in-exile.

Mr Quill nodded and sat down. He was so shocked he did not know what to say.

'No point in keeping things in too long, is what I always say,' laughed Miss Lee gaily.

'Except sometimes,' said Murphy.

'Isn't he sweet, dear.' Miss Lee patted Mr Quill's hand.

'Blessed are the peacemakers for they shall inherit the kingdom of heaven,' said Murphy, with a lascivious glance at Miss Lee's well-exposed bosom.

'What'll you have, dear?'

'I'll have a pint,' said Mr Quill, disengaging himself. 'It's hot weather.'

'You can say that again,' said Murphy.

'Naughty boy. I can see that this is no place for an innocent young girl like me.'

'A pint,' said Mr Quill to the barman, who stood looking down at him with his hand on his hip, his bright golden hair elaborately dressed, indistinguishable in every particular, except for his white jacket, from the young men who clustered about the juke-box, swaying their hips and snapping their fingers to the rhythm.

'Are you not able to drink whiskey?' said Murphy,

raising his glass and looking at Iris pointedly over its brim.

'What do you mean am I not able to drink whiskey? Of course I'm able to drink whiskey. It's just that I feel like having a pint. And if I feel like having a pint I have a pint.'

'I never saw you drinking whiskey in Mick's. All those, years Paul drank it and you drank Guinness. A hard man, Paul.'

'Do I bring whiskey or do I bring a pint?' said the barman in a deep contralto voice.

Mr Quill had exactly thirty shillings left until his next pay-cheque in a week's time. Enough to buy a reasonable number of pints to kill the long golden summer evenings.

'My friend will have a pint,' said Miss Lee.

'Bring whiskey,' said Mr Quill firmly. 'And bring two more for the company.'

'Heaven, dear,' cried Iris, clapping her hands. 'I'm glad I decided to break the gin habit. I can see this is going to be a good evening.'

'Get you,' said Murphy.

'And get you too, dear. I bet you can't down whiskey like my Johnny here. I've seen him drinking a whole bottle and it didn't knock a feather out of him.'

'Chicken-feed,' said Murphy.

'I never saw you drinking whiskey,' said Mr Quill, who was beginning to be angry.

'There's a lot of things you never saw me doing. Isn't that right Iris?'

'I should hope not, dear.'

The barman came back with the whiskey.

'Bring me another round,' said Murphy. 'Doubles this time. I'm not accustomed to drinking small whiskies.'

After that they had another round, and then another. Neither Mr Quill or Murphy, mindful of their celebrated battle, would allow Miss Lee to pay. Soon Mr Quill's thirty shillings was reduced to nothing; but he went on lowering drink for drink with his antagonist. Miss Lee, watching the contest, which she imagined to be a tribute to her charms, instead of a competition in vanity, sipped her drinks carefully, and allowed them to accumulate in neat rows in front of her. She did not want to be drunk when the time came to congratulate her champion, which, to give her her due, she confidently hoped and expected would be Mr Quill.

But he had no money left. He was spared the indignity of withdrawing from the contest, because the barman came to collect for the last round while Murphy was paying a visit to the famous men's room.

'Oh, my God,' he exclaimed in genuine horror, 'I left the rest of my money at home.'

'No, you didn't leave it at home, dear,' said Iris with great presence of mind. 'You gave it to me to mind this afternoon, remember?' And opening her handbag she took out two five-pound notes, and folded them tenderly in Mr Quill's palm. Not a moment too soon, for Murphy came staggering back to his seat while Mr Quill was still staring in amazement at his clenched fist, which held such dishonourable riches.

'Pay up, dear,' said Miss Lee, looking at her reflection in her hand-mirror and preparing to powder her nose. 'It's your round. You're always giving out about how a lady ought never to pay. Well, this is my night out.'

Mr Quill opened his hand slowly and looked down at the two crisp pieces of paper. Then he looked at Miss Lee, who was watching him steadily over her powder-puff. Half drunk though he was, he understood what her glance implied. This, his instincts told him, is how the world goes round. I could make money this way. And he thought in a muddled sort of way about the seventy pound she owed Philip; and all the bills Sybil had run up and were still unpaid. With the temptation came the realization of something he would never have allowed himself to think about if he had been sober. The world was not as beautiful as he imagined; love was not a romantic charade played to soft music; men and women could be bought and sold: above all that was what most of them wanted. He saw it in the small triumphant smile on Miss Lee's lips as she powdered her nose. He heard it in the raucous music of the juke-box. He recognized it in the greedy eyes of the barman, whose gaze was fixed boldly, with a sort of calculating deference, on Mr Quill's face.

'Is there anything particular you want, sir ?' he asked in a creamy voice.

'Pay the boy his money,' said Miss Lee, snapping her compact shut. 'Something tells me he's a very busy boy indeed.'

Mr Quill made no move. He was paralysed with disgust, and a sort of chaotic longing that he could not understand. Miss Lee leaned over and took one of the notes, which she handed to the barman.

'Are you sick ?' said Murphy. 'Are you not able to take it ? Not a whiskey drinker, after all.'

'Excuse me,' said Mr Quill, getting up and leaving the other five-pound note on the table. 'I'm not a bit sick, but I want to pay a visit to the toilet for the same reason as yourself. And when I come back we'll have another round, which will be on you.'

Inside the lavatory, surrounded by the celebrated *graffiti*, he was sick. He was not used to drinking whiskey; but his sickness was of a more serious kind. He was sick with himself. For he knew that he wanted Miss Lee's money very much; not only the ten pounds she had given him, but the promise of so much more that lay in her eyes. And the thought occurred to him that he might be able to get the money without becoming involved with her too much; and he became sicker still, until his disgust with himself, and the Green Bar and Miss Lee and the wreck of his romantic dreams lay at his feet in a froth of vomit.

When he had splashed his face with water he felt a little better. He knew what he was going to do. He would take the money—since he could not return it with Murphy looking on—and return it when he got his cheque. He did not allow himself to dwell on the fact that he would certainly spend all of it before pay-day; nor did he consider that when that day came he would be quite unable to take ten pounds out of an already heavily mortgaged amount. But for the moment his resolution was firm; his hopes high; his faith undaunted. He had fought the good fight against the withering forces of reality; and he returned to the bar as triumphantly as he had come back from his battle with Murphy.

But for some reason he could not bring himself to touch the money, and addressed himself heavily to his whiskey. Miss Lee sensed his reticence and took action. She picked up the five-pound note, and the change which lay beside it, and slipped them into his pocket, allowing herself to give him a playful little pat on the thigh.

'I wouldn't be so careless about my money if I were you, dear,' she said with mock severity.

Mr Quill said nothing. There was nothing to do except order another round.

'Were you sick in there?' said Murphy. He felt that the contest was going against him, and badly wanted to fall asleep.

'No,' said Mr Quill, 'were you?'

'I'm not drunk, there's nothing drunk about me.' Then his head fell heavily onto his chest and he began to snore quietly.

'Gracious,' said Miss Lee wrinkling her nose with disgust, 'snuffed out like a candle. And he told me he never drank anything but malt in his life. I like that I must say.' She turned to Mr Quill with a brilliant smile, ready to receive the reward which experience had taught her is often accomplished by the discreet disposal of ten pounds cash. But both her champions failed her. Mr Quill had won the contest; but he was in no condition to reap its rewards. He was staring straight in front of him with glassy eyes. His ruddy complexion had faded and was tinged with green. He lifted his finger slowly inch by inch and waved it in front of his mouth. He was stoned.

'Are you all right, dear?' Miss Lee leaned forward and grasped his knee firmly.

Mr Quill grunted, and placed his finger on his lip. Then slowly, quietly, his eyelids drooped, his head fell; and Miss Lee, for whom the evening had begun with such bright promise, was left with two insensible men on her hands. And with seven unfinished double whiskies in front of her. These however did not go to waste; for ten minutes before closing-time, as if directed by the sweet smell of them, Paul came in. The recumbent figures received scant attention from; but the sight of such untasted riches caused his eyes to open as wide as if he had seen a vision of eternity.

'In the name of all the holy sinners of Dublin who's leaving all that malt behind them?' he said in a horrified voice.

'Me,' said Iris.

Paul took his book from under his arm, seized a chair, put his book on it and sat down with alacrity: for there were now only eight minutes to closing time.

'Gather ye rosebuds,' said he, grasping the first glass, 'while ye may.'

15

SNIP went Miss Blake's scissors. Beyond the rose-beds the two milk-bottles, hung up side by side from the branch of a tree to frighten the birds away from the strawberries, clicked gently together in the evening breeze. A clouded yellow butterfly spun for a moment like a halo about the old lady's head, and then fluttered away. All was quiet except for the humming of bees, the tinkle of the bottles, and the snip-snip of the scissors. Miss Blake was gathering her roses. And behind her, carrying a basket already half-full with scarlet blooms as richly coloured as drops of blood, walked Sybil Quill.

Miss Blake paused beside a bed of yellow roses with delicate pink-shaded petals.

'This is my Peace bed. It's my pride and joy, because I was the first person in Ireland to grow them. I got them from France before they were brought to England. That was in 1942. Smuggled in, dear, in a diplomatic bag. Not that I'm gone on yellow roses. No,' she went on, bending and cutting lustily, 'red roses for me.'

She held up one of the yellow roses and inhaled its scent greedily.

'You see it's not all yellow. It's got that subtle pink shading. That's what I love, having your cake and eating it.'

She pointed to a bed of dazzling vermilion roses, shining like painted china in the sun.

'Look at those. Super Star, raised only last year in Germany. Aren't they absolutely thrilling?'

She moved on.

'Ah, but this is my real treasure, my Crimson Glories. It hurts me even to cut them. It's like killing one's own children, if you know what I mean,' She bent down and proceeded to fill Sybil's basket with Crimson Glories. Then she straightened herself up with a groan. 'You know, I want to have a bowl of those by me when I'm dying. They're the last thing I want to look at, the last beautiful memory. For that reason I know I'll never die in the winter, but in the summer when all my children are in bloom. God wouldn't be cruel enough to refuse an old woman such a simple request.' She pointed her scissors at Sybil. 'And I give you permission to pull one of them after I'm gone and place it on my grave. Will you promise to do that?'

Sybil did not look up from her basket of roses. She was crying.

'Well, will you or won't you?'

'Yes, Miss Blake,' whispered Sybil.

'I've asked all my friends to pluck one and place it on my grave. I wonder how many of them will. That's one way of getting to know your friends.' She chuckled and sliced the air with her scissors. 'I think we've cut enough, dear. Let's sit down here for a few minutes.'

She led the way to a rustic seat placed under a sycamore tree. Behind them the milk-bottles tinkled like distant bells. It was a sound Sybil was to remember for the rest of her life. The sound of early morning. The sound of waking up. She put down her basket by her feet and stared dully in front of her.

Miss Blake settled her shapeless hat with one hand, and placed the other with its great emerald on Sybil's arm.

'Now, dear, you mustn't worry too much about what I've just told you. That's why I thought I'd ask you to help me cut the roses. It takes your mind off things. You have no idea what a comfort my rose children are to me when I'm in trouble. And I want them to be the same to you.'

'I can't believe it.'

'That's what I said when I heard it first, dear. The whole thing is quite shocking. But I'm afraid it's true, because I made certain enquiries, and there is no doubt at all in my mind. So you must be brave and face up to it for your daughter's sake. As I did for yours.'

'It's very kind of you, Miss Blake.' Sybil could think of nothing to say, except repeat the banal phrases which had helped her through life hitherto.

'Of course it's not kind of me. I'm simply acting as a friend should. I don't want to see your daughter's life ruined. I'm not like Mrs Jellyby. I believe that charity should begin at home.' She took a long-stemmed Crimson Glory from the basket and sniffed it. The bottles tinkled behind them; and the warm breeze surrounded them with the scent of the blazing beds. 'I only told you because sooner or later you'd hear it from somebody else. They'd tell you out of spite, just to watch your face. Oh, I know Dublin. So you might as well be prepared. It's really the kindest thing in the end.' She shifted in her seat and held the rose against her bosom.

'But what am I going to tell John? Philip O'Connor is his best friend.'

Miss Blake sniffed her rose again, and looked at Sybil's anguished face over the dark crimson petals. For a moment she was tempted. But like Mr Quill himself she was in her way an artist. Never too much of a good thing; a delicate feeling for mood and probability: these were the characteristics of her besetting vice. She would tell Sybil about her husband later, when the effects of this first bombshell had begun to wear off. And there was so much to tell. The man was making an absolute disgrace of himself. Only a few nights before he had had to be carried out dead drunk from the lowest bar in the town—for Miss Blake knew everything—with that cheap blonde in tow. That was something that must be saved up for one of those flat periods when nothing seemed to be happening.

'Tell him the truth, dear. It's better that he should hear it from you than from some stranger. Besides, Philip is rather a well-known man, and Dublin is a large village, and sooner or later everybody is going to know about it. Indeed it's already being spoken about.'

'Oh, no it couldn't be.' Sybil's voice lost its vague, tremulous tone, and became sharp. She seemed for the first time to be really listening to what the old woman was saying, instead of meekly submitting to some sort of intolerable sentence which she did not quite believe in. Miss Blake shot her a sharp glance, and pursed her lips. Behind them the bottles suddenly banged together with a loud clatter.

'The wind is changing. It always does with my mood, like Mr Jarndyce.'

'Mr Who?' Sybil's faculties, screwed now to fever pitch by the thought of public disclosure which she had been too stunned to consider before, fastened upon this strange name, which seemed to her in her bewildered state to be in some way connected with the unspeakable thing which she had just been told.

'Mr Jarndyce is a character in a novel by Charles Dickens. You know I'm a great reader.' *Bleak House* was the only novel of Dickens that Miss Blake had ever managed to finish, having been marooned with it during a wet week in the West of Ireland, and she had a quotation for every occasion.

'Oh, said Sybil with a sigh of relief, 'I thought it might be somebody who knows.'

'Well, you know it's been going on for some time now. Dublin being what it is I'm afraid quite a lot of people know. I've known it for some time, and I suppose I should have told you at the beginning, but one doesn't want to interfere. That was one thing my mother always told me, and I've never forgotten it. My mother was a very wise woman. Of course, you don't have to take my word for it.'

'I didn't mean it like that, Miss Blake,' said Sybil hastily, sensing the annoyance in the old woman's voice, and eager now for all the information she could get.

'As it is I'm taking a great risk in telling you, and you may never speak to me again, but right is right, and if you have a true friend you ought to tell them the truth, that's what I always say.' The old lady thumped her hat again and stuck her nose angrily into her rose.

'It's very good of you, Miss Blake, it really is, and I appreciate it.' Sybil turned round and stared imploringly at the massive grey profile beside her. But Miss Blake's eye was closed, and her mouth and nose were nuzzling the flower moodily. 'I'd never have heard it if it wasn't for you.'

'Yes, you would,' snappped Miss Blake. 'You'd have heard it when it was too late to do anything from some kind neighbour coming out of the church. Please remember that these people, the O'Connors, are friends of mine too. And now that I've taken you into my confidence I expect the same confidence from you.'

'Of course Miss Blake. I wouldn't dream—'

'But the really shocking thing about it is the place he brings her to, because it was there that Philip met his wife and proposed to her. I suppose I'm sentimental—' she broke off and peered across the garden to where a dumpy figure in black wearing a white apron was walking towards them. 'Good heavens, what does Anderson want now? She's always looking for something, the old cow.'

Sybil bent down and picked up the basket of roses quickly. As she huddled over it a tear ran down her cheek, and dropped on the soft petal of a Crimson Glory.

'Well, Anderson, what do you want?'

Over the years the housekeeper had grown very like her mistress: the same shapeless figure, the rolling gait, the yellow-white hair, the discoloured teeth, the sly, malicious eyes.

'There's a man at the door collecting for one of those Catholic Pools,' she said. Her voice was the voice of Miss Blake, fat, wheezy, and complaining. 'We owe him two shillings. You weren't here when he called last week.'

'I haven't got my bag. It's on my dressing-table. Go and see if there's any money in it. I always seem to be paying out, but I notice I never win. I suppose these things are rigged, like everything else.'

'I looked in your bag.' Anderson studied Sybil's bent head with attention. 'There's nothing in it. Maybe—' the voice adopted a soft wheedling note—'Mrs Quill has some change on her.'

'Sybil, dear, have you any change on you?'

Sybil groped in the pocket of her cardigan, where she had a few shillings left out of her housekeeping money. While she fumbled with the money, dropping a sixpence into the basket of roses, the two old women looked at her

99

with sharp anxious eyes, the corners of their mouths twitching with identical greed. Sybil found a two-shilling piece and handed it to Miss Blake without looking up.

'The same man, I suppose, Anderson?'

'A friend of Mr Quill's, I believe,' said the housekeeper, snatching the money from her mistress. 'Devotes his life to charity.'

They cackled with identical laughter. Then Anderson waddled away, and Miss Blake laid her grimy hand on Sybil's arm.

'Now dear you must bear up.'

'I'm all right, Miss Blake, really I am. It's just the shock.'

'However don't do anything hasty. Talk it over with your husband.'

'But Philip O'Connor—' burst out Sybil.

'Yes, indeed, dear. When you get to my age nothing that any man can do will surprise you. Do you know that only a few years ago I came into my own kitchen and found that man who collects for the raffles, the man your husband has a drink with now and again, kissing Anderson. Anderson, at her age! Can you imagine it? That's how he gets his subscriptions. No wonder he's so successful. Upon my word there are times when humanity disgusts me.' She paused and took the basket from Sybil's lap and replaced the rose she had been clutching to her bosom. 'Is Caroline out tonight, dear?'

'Yes, she went out after tea. She went to the tennis club.'

'Well, Jim Ashton is in the 'phone book. I don't think I told you the name of the house. It's "Moytura". I think if you rang up about ten o'clock Philip might answer.'

Sybil stood up. Her long pale face was streaked with tears. She looked blindly across the blood-red garden, and heard faintly as if from very far off the little tinkle of the empty milk-bottles.

'I must go,' she blurted out.

'Yes, dear. It's getting late. Tell me how things work out won't you? And remember, I told you nothing.'

Sybil nodded.

'And here, take one of these.' Miss Blake picked up one of the flaming roses and handed it to Sybil. 'A little present from an old woman.'

Sybil hurried off down the path that led to the side-gate, clutching her red rose in her hands. Miss Blake watched her go with a little smile. The contentment that she felt was not light-hearted or frivolous; but the dark, sensual joy of those whose instincts have turned inward and become destructive. She was humming to herself as she picked up her basket and went back towards the house, touching a rose here and there, as she might the cheek of a sleeping child. She was wondering if she might be in time to catch Anderson playing her monstrous game with Paul. Miss Blake had often listened with keen interest in the passage outside the kitchen to the strange sounds that came from within. She quickened her steps. The flaming blooms winked and dipped as she passed in her dusty black, dragging her shadow like a ragged shawl behind her. And the empty bottles tolled in the gathering shadows.

16

THIS also was love, and these the identical signs. The racing of the heart that arose not from passion but anxiety; the sweat that was the result of fear, not satiety; the anger that clouded the mind no less than desire. And this the same time: the hour that passed so luminously in love-making, that now dragged so heavily.

Caroline walked back and forward across the lawn, unaware as the time passed of the shadow of the house as she once had been. It seemed to her that the place, which had always seemed so silent, was now full of sounds. Not the noises that she had taken for granted, like the singing of birds, the hum of motor-cars on the road outside; but echoes. She became aware of the rustling of birds in the shrubbery; of the ghostly sighing of the laburnum against the wall of the house; of the ripple of leaves; and the bony creaking of old trees. And once, quite near her as she passed under one of the great beeches, a tiny tapping sound—the same sound her father had heard on the day he had visited Philip: the pecking of a thrush killing a snail against a stone. Then as she walked under the terrace she stopped in terror, listening to a sound from the house: a far-off, insistent echo of something familiar, and yet in that place, at that time, more frightening than the known. She stood quite still holding her elbows tightly against her breasts, listening to the telephone ringing in the empty hall. It was only when the stiletto stabs of sound had ceased that she remembered that Philip had given her a key of the house; and that she should have answered it. He was already an hour late; and he was ringing to tell her. Philip had never been late before. He had always been there waiting for her. His presence had helped her to overcome her instinctive fear of the old place, in which every piece of furniture seemed to watch her with distrust. It was like finding oneself in a room with a paralysed stranger who is unable to speak; but whose eyes glitter with suspicion.

She turned away and walked quickly across the shadowed lawn and down the avenue. She stood inside the gates for a few minutes looking out on the roads. It was like all the roads in Killiney, steep and hilly; and a party of young people in bright frocks and flannels were walking their bicycles up the incline at the end of the lane. One or two of them looked at the young girl standing inside the iron gates; and then passed on, breathless, laughing, and free. Caroline went and sat down on the steps of the lodge, clutching her knees in her arms, listening to the ticking of her wristwatch. She made up her mind to wait for another ten minutes.

But he did not come for half an hour; and she was still waiting; standing now huddled against the doorway of the lodge. He saw her as he opened the gates, and hurried over to her.

'Are you cold?' He took her hands in his and pressed them.

'No.'

'Your hands are freezing.'

'My hands are always cold.'

'It's chilly this evening. Why didn't you go into the house?'

'I'm not cold.'

She followed him silently into the car, and they drove up the short avenue to the house. He stopped the car and turned to take her in his arms.

'No,' she said, drawing away and huddling against the corner of the seat.

'I'm sorry I'm late. Some friends called from home just as I was leaving, and I couldn't get away from them.' Like Mr Quill, Philip always spoke of the midland town in which they had been born as 'home'.

'I don't mind waiting.'

'They're relatives of mine actually. Third cousins or something. You know how it is in the country, everybody is related to everybody else.'

With his presence some of her fear left her. He reached out and took her hand.

'Will it always be like this, Philip?'

'I've never been late before.' He took her other hand, and held them tightly to give them warmth.

'It isn't that. I don't mind waiting. But will I always be afraid when you're not with me?'

'Why should you be afraid? You have nothing to be afraid of. I'm the one who should be afraid.'

'When are those people coming back? I mean the people who own the house.'

'A few weeks' time.'

'We should never have come here,' she burst out. 'I hate it. I've always hated it.'

Instead of grasping her hands more tightly, and reassuring her with that kind of brutal self-confidence that fears respond to, he released her gently and turned away, looking at the old house standing in its shadows. He seemed suddenly remote and preoccupied.

'No, we shouldn't have come here. I know that. But you have nothing to fear from this house. You're too young to be afraid of anything.'

'You have taught me to be afraid,' she said with deliberate cruelty. Fear preys upon fear. The balance of their relationship had rested on her complete trust. It would never have occurred to her that Philip could have been afraid of anything. She did not think of him as old; but as infallible. This, she thought in the beginning, is what love is; because Philip knows. The tenderness before love-making; the gentle insistence of the act; the deferment of pleasure until it became a sensual release only he could bestow: all that was love, because Philip had revealed it to her. There was no other; and for her there never would be. No crude, healthy mating of innocent young bodies; no laughter, no sudden explosion of wild gaiety; no fumbling towards a sweet and mutual wonderment. Love was secret as a shadow in a dusty mirror; love was solitary as the silent rooms of a deserted house; love did not pass by sweating and loud-voiced on a summer road. Love stood behind a gate in the shade of old trees and a shuttered house. Love was a mask of indifference one wore in the presence of others; a mask which she did not know sometimes slips. Love was fugitive; fearful of the past, uncertain of the future. Love was fear; a fear she had been able to face because she knew that Philip could never share it. He was the certainty that youth seeks. She had clung to him as a child will shelter in the shadow of its father.

Now as he turned back to her his face was drawn; older than she had ever seen it before. She did not realize that she was beginning to see him for the first time; and that the little space that separated them between the seats of the car was the distance of many years.

'I'm sorry,' he said sadly.

For a moment she felt a clawing desire to wound him. But the menace of the world outside restrained her: the world without Philip, in which she had allowed herself to become a stranger. Better the pain of being with him than the numbness of being alone. He had become a necessity.

'Oh, Philip, we mustn't quarrel. It's all my fault. I'm sorry. Don't let's sit here any longer. It's getting late, and there isn't much time left.'

Inside the house it was now almost dark. In the drawing-room Caroline went over to the bowl of roses which she had picked a few days earlier in the garden. They stood now in a pool of petals, like the roses she had seen the first evening she had come to the house. She touched one of them that was still unwithered: it dissolved under her fingers, and the petals fluttered down about her feet. She turned and ran into Philip's arms.

'Oh, I was so afraid waiting here for you. I don't mind when you're with me, but I could never come here alone. I couldn't even pluck up enough courage to come in and answer the 'phone when you rang. It was awful listening to it out there on the lawn. But you didn't have to ring. I knew you'd come.'

Philip took her arms from his shoulders and held them against his chest. 'The 'phone. Did the 'phone ring while you were waiting?'

'Yes, of course. It was you ringing to tell me that you'd be late. It was stupid of me to be afraid.' She leaned her forehead against his shoulder.

'No, Caroline, it wasn't me.'

She snatched her hands from him and started back.

'But I heard the 'phone ring. I stood listening out there under the terrace. I could hear it distinctly.'

'I didn't ring.'

For a moment Caroline was confused. Then she began to be angry.

'No, of course,' she said, turning away from him. 'Why should you? You were so sure I'd be waiting. You could quite easily have 'phoned me. A few words would have done. But no, you had nothing to worry about.'

'But you didn't answer the 'phone, Caroline,' he said wearily. 'You said you wouldn't come into the house.'

'I thought it was you. At the time I knew it was you. That's all that mattered. You could have stopped at the first box when you left your house. Did you think of that?'

'No. I wanted to get here as quickly as I could. Caroline, please——'

'Leave me alone.'

She stepped away from his outstretched arm, and began to gather the fallen petals where they lay about the rose-bowl. They were brittle and curled at the edges like autumn leaves. She scooped them into her palm and threw them into the empty fireplace. He made no move to follow her, but stood staring in the dim light at the drawn blinds. Suddenly she became furious. The crumpling of his authority that had shocked her in the car had given her the taste of blood. She could no longer restrain the desire to wound him; as we always seek to wound those in whom we create an image that we seek, when for a brief moment by an unspoken word, a trembling hand, the flicker of an eyelid, they reveal the truth, and the image dissolves like a withered rose. She could not forgive Philip for sharing her fear.

But above all she was preparing herself, as people always unconsciously do, for the future. We live only partly in the present: the past moulds it; and for those who stumble blindly into love, which has its own sorcery, the future is sometimes revealed. They rehearse it unknowingly in the timelessness of their obsession.

'Caroline,' he begged, repeating her own words, 'we mustn't quarrel. It's all my fault. I'm sorry.'

'You aren't sorry. You just don't want to be inconvenienced. Oh, you had it all so well planned. An empty house. A few hours with me whenever you could spare the time. And if you're an hour or two late what does it matter?'

'All right, we won't meet here any more. I know you don't like it. But it seemed the only place—'

'To make love, yes. That was the only thing that mattered, wasn't it? How many others have you brought here? And is this the way it began to end? Give them the key and keep them waiting. A hint in time.'

Suddenly the room was flooded with light. Caroline cried out and covered her face with her hands. Philip had moved to the door and switched on the great glass chandelier that hung from a carved plaque in the centre of the ceiling. Outside on the darkening lawn the block of light fell upon the shadows.

'I have brought no one here, no one but you. I brought you here because I loved you. Because you're young and unspoiled and innocent. Yes, innocent. Would you have preferred me to bring you to an hotel? There are plenty of that kind in Dublin. I could have displayed you publicly as my mistress. My young, my very young mistress.' Philip's voice was hard with anger; and when Caroline took her hands from her eyes and looked at him, she could see that his face was white and trembling. A middle-aged man from whom the mask of imperturbability had fallen.

'Put out the light,' she said, holding up her hands in front of her narrowed eyes.

'No.'

They were not quarrelling about a telephone call. They were wrestling with despair, and the hopelessness of the future, which obscurely they were seeking to anticipate.

They faced each other in the light of the winking crystals, which seemed after the darkness almost a glare—like the headlamps of a passing car sweeping across two lovers huddled by a wall. Caroline was the first to surrender. She ran sobbing into his arms. He held her roughly, pinning her arms against her sides, digging his fingers into the bare flesh below her elbows. She cried out, not with pain, but with a sort of pleasure. Those dry searching lips, that hard ruthless body were all that were left of certainty.

'Put out the light,' she begged.

'No, Caroline. This time we are going to see each other. It's time you did. After all I might be a leper.'

All tenderness gone they made use of each other, seeking in violence a substitute for the faith she had lost, the certainty he had never had. The hard diamonds of light flickered over naked limbs harshly twined in the motions of love; the motions that are the same for the dumb, the blind, the happy, the despairing, the sensualist and the cynic: the ultimately comic coupling of self-deceiving flesh. Exposed to the swaying light Caroline and Philip were funny.

And then while they lay numb, exhausted and bathed in sweat, the telephone rang again.

'Don't answer it,' she whispered.

'We'll have to answer it sometime,' he said, rising wearily and leaving her. While he was away she hurriedly began to dress. She was almost finished when he came back. But she saw nothing comic in the sight of the slight naked figure with dishevelled hair standing in the doorway. She turned instinctively away from him, holding her cheap cotton frock against her breast.

'They know,' he said in a dead voice.

17

SYBIL QUILL was proud of her address. The red-brick terrace house seemed to her the summit of respectability because it had two windows on the ground floor, one on either side of the door. Sybil firmly believed that one window below and two above put a house in a class not far removed from a council terrace. Nor was she displeased with the people who were her neighbours: civil servants for the most part, there was not an uncollared worker among them. She had made discreet enquiries before she bought the house; and in the twenty years that she had lived there the proper tone had been kept up. A few families had moved out, and others had taken their places, so alike in income, habit and number of progeny that they might have been the same people. If Sybil had been an observant person she might have noticed the little signs of wear and tear that the years of inflation had brought: the frayed collar, the turned suit, the dyed curtain. She would have been aware of the bitterness in the eyes of some of the women of her own age; of a certain false jauntiness in the bearing of the men who went to their offices, schools, and family shops in the morning. She would, if she had made friends with any of them, have been very much surprised at the vicious resentment some of them felt at the burden of respectability which they were forced to bear on incomes which were always just a little inadequate.

But Sybil had had her legacy. She had not moved with the times. And her standards had been formed in the kitchen living-room behind her father's butcher's shop. The people she had lived among since her marriage were the people who had lived in semi-detached villas in the suburbs of her native town: she had always vaguely envied them, as her parents had done. They were respectable, professional people who worked in offices, served on church committees, and were pensionable. Of the really rich like the O'Connors, or the remains of the Ascendancy like Miss Blake, she felt no envy at all. It is always the next step in the social hierarchy that people resent, and strive to achieve. In her trim brick house, with its front and back gardens, its garage, its four windows facing the road, and its tiny cell at the top of the stairs intended as a maid's room, Sybil had achieved her heart's desire.

But now, as she stood looking out of her drawing-room window she reverted to type. The terrace was no longer the embodiment of a harmless dream: it was the street in which she had been born and reared, A narrow street, curving down a hill towards a river, with high stark houses rising above the fronts of pubs, family grocers, sweet-shops, grain-merchants, and the other butcher's that was her father's obsession. A street in which everything was known; where the first signs of illness on an ageing face were watched as closely, and as secretly, as some obscene rite followed by a *voyeur*; where the slighest departure from the accepted norm was welcomed, because the little hypocritical fuss it provoked was the only diversion that the street could ever experience. Sybil had grown up in an atmosphere in which one was not sorry for doing wrong because it was sinful, but because it exposed one to ridicule. She had heard the whispering, the muffled laughter, the raucous merriment; and she had never forgotten them.

And so when she had heard about Caroline and Philip O'Connor she did not—after the shock had worn off—vacillate as she often did when confronted with the boring details of day-to-day living. She acted swiftly and with resolution, as her mother would have acted if Sybil had allowed herself to be seen home from a dance by a married man. She looked up James Ashton's number in the 'phone book and rang it. When Philip answered she had not pretended to know him: she had merely told him briefly that she knew her daughter was in the house and that she wanted her home immediately. Then she rang Mick's, where she knew her husband always drank in the evenings with Paul, and told him with the same new-found curt authority that she wanted him home at once. She did not know that Mr Quill had forsaken Mick's for some time in favour of the Green Bar; or that he had returned to his old haunt again only a few nights before, having given up avoiding Miss Lee now that he was in her debt. She knew with the certainty of her blood that he would be there; and he was.

Now she drew the curtains, although it was not yet dark, and switched on the lights. A light showing through a chink in the curtains in a family living-room was, she knew with the wisdom of the old street, a beacon held up against the onslaughts of the outside world. In trouble: in death, sickness, and fear of discovery, one put on the lights. Then she made herself a cup of tea and sat down to wait.

Mr Quill was the first to arrive. He had spent a good evening at Mick's where Miss Lee told him that there was no hurry about paying back the money. He had been very insistent about his intention to pay it back: Miss Lee had been equally insistent that it was nothing at all. These protestations had been made before Paul came in; after which the three of them settled down to the more serious business of spending more money on drink. It did not seem to Mr Quill that anything unpleasant could happen on such an agreeable evening; and when Sybil 'phoned it did not unduly disturb his state of mind. But it was necessary to invent some excuse for leaving the company at such an early hour. He therefore decided that some cousins from home had arrived. He described these relatives in such detail to Miss Lee and Paul that he confidently expected them to be sitting in the living-room when he got home. It was something of a shock to find his wife alone, with the curtains half drawn and the lights on, although it was not yet dark.

'I thought the Kellys were here,' he said, looking around

the tiny room with narrowed eyes, as if he expected to find them hiding behind the furniture.

'The Kellys?' Sybil, who had carefully rehearsed what she was going to say to her husband, was put off course, and stared at him in amazement.

'Yes, Bill and Nell from home. Aren't they here?'

'Of course they're not here. Who told you that?'

'But I thought that's why you asked me to come home. I thought Bill and Nell had dropped in.'

'I didn't say a single word about the Kellys,' said Sybil sharply. 'I don't know what gave you that idea. Have you been drinking?'

This was a question which she had never asked her husband in the whole of her married life. She accepted the fact that a man should go out every evening for a drink with his friends as part of the immutable order of the universe; and would have been somewhat embarrassed if he had offered to stay at home and wash up. That was something Sybil knew no respectable Irishman should ever be asked to do. Men were men and women were women. They came together for a brief period in the marriage bed; something that a woman had to put up with, since that too was part of the order of the universe. Otherwise the less time they spent together the better, in her opinion.

But tonight these ancient, artificial social conventions, common to Catholic countries, collapsed, and she reverted to a still more ancient and more inexorable standard: fear of the unknown.

Mr Quill sat down suddenly and stared at his wife.

'Of course I've been drinking,' he said in a hurt voice. 'You know very well that I have two pints with Paul every evening. It's the only break I get.'

'And a couple of whiskeys too from the smell of you,' snapped Sybil.

'No such thing. There was only Paul and myself.' Mr Quill prepared himself for a long recital of what he and

Paul had talked about. Paul in fact had said very little. Miss Lee carried the conversation; but Mr Quill began to feel a little uneasy about her in the presence of his wife. The bond established for the price of ten pounds was beginning to tighten.

'Well, while you were out boozing you might be interested to know what has happened to your daughter.' On most occasions when Sybil talked about Caroline she called her 'my daughter' or 'our daughter'. Now quite unconsciously it seemed to her that Caroline was her father's daughter. As she launched into a recital of what Miss Blake had told her, she contrived to give the impression that Caroline's disgrace was entirely her father's fault. He was never at home when he should be. And most important of all Philip was his friend, not Sybil's.

While she spoke Mr Quill sat very quietly, trying to collect his thoughts. As a child taken to see a corpse for the first time will not believe that it could ever have been a living human being, and will accept it quite calmly as something outside the course of nature; so too Mr Quill found the story Sybil was telling him impossible to believe. It was as if he had gone into his office one morning and found it entirely staffed by apes: such a thing could not happen.

When she finished Sybil covered her eyes with her hands and began to weep. It had not occurred to her for a single moment to doubt Miss Blake's word. Like all women she accepted bad news quicker than good; and she found it easy to believe anything of those she loved.

Mr Quill's reactions were different. He did not think it possible that a daughter of his could be so abandoned; a daughter that he loved so much that she had always reduced him to the humility of silence. Male vanity is so great that it cannot accept any fault in the objects of its affections. Philip O'Connor was the golden friend of his youth; and Mr Quill always invested his friends with something of his own childish innocence. And so at the moment he was not so much disturbed by his wife's story as by her complete change of attitude. Sybil had never acted like this before. He was puzzled; and so he began to bluster.

'Who's this Miss Blake anyhow?' he said roughly. 'You're always talking about her. You'd imagine she was the Queen. You'd be better off if you stayed at home and minded your own business instead of listening to some dirty-minded old bitch like that.'

It did not occur to Sybil that without his spectacles her husband could not see her tears. It was this seeming heartlessness on his part rather than his actual words that now roused her to fury. She jumped up, shaking with hysterical rage.

'How dare you speak like that in my house,' she screamed. 'You're not in some filthy bar now boozing with your low-down friends. If it hadn't been for Miss Blake we might never have heard of the way your great Philip O'Connor had taken advantage of Caroline. Miss Blake is a better friend to me than any you've ever had. What do you mean by calling her a filthy name? Answer me that.'

'I'll call her what I like, if that's the sort she is, spreading dirty lies about my daughter. I'm surprised that you wouldn't be ashamed to listen to her. Don't you know that the country is full of old cats like that, who spend their whole time spreading gossip and scandal about everybody Many's the time I heard you say that if you only walked home from the Sodality with a man they'd have you in the ditch with him next morning.'

'I never walked home from the women's Sodality with anybody except women,' said Sybil, her rage abating as she felt the necessity of defending herself.

'That's not what you told me.'

'Well, I'm telling you now.'

'And how about the time you got a lift to Dublin with that commercial traveller. What did they say about you then? Answer me that. Didn't they say—'

'I never went to Dublin with a commercial traveller in my life,' cried Sybil. 'I'd like to see my mother's face if I suggested such a thing.'

'You didn't tell her. You met him outside the Royal Hotel, and when you got back in the evening on the bus the whole town knew it. At any rate that's what you told me.'

'I told you no such thing. Just because you spend every night of your life boozing with that Paul, and haven't time to spend a minute with your wife and daughter, you try to cover yourself by making up stories like that. If you were half a man you'd go up to this house in Killiney, and find out if your daughter is there with your so-called friend.'

'I think more of my daughter and of my friends too than to believe every bit of tittle-tattle that I hear from gossipy old women. I don't know what Phil must think of you ringing up like that, and telling him to send Caroline home. He must have thought you had gone out of your mind. And ringing me up too in Mick's where Paul was giving me a tip about the Pools, and frightening the life out of me about the Kellys.'

And so they wrangled, backing away from a subject they really wanted to avoid. Unaware also that the comic walks side by side with the tragic; and sometimes precedes it, as the shadow of the hangman covers the ground before him with a grotesque reflection of his implacable figure. People are never so ludicrous as in those brief hysterical moments before the most tragic events of their lives when, warned by some instinct, they dance recklessly upon the precipice. The clown is a more sinister figure of doom than the raven.

It was Sybil who brought the conversation back to reality.

'Very well,' she said, 'wait until Caroline gets home. She should be here any minute now. If she comes we'll know that she was in that house with your friend.'

Then she sat down with a frozen face, withdrawing herself mentally from her husband, and feeling for him something of that hate women always feel towards their men, when at the moment of necessity, in preparation for which a wife imagines she has spent her whole life ministering to a husband she really regards as a child, she finds that in fact she is talking to a child.

But Caroline did not come. As the minutes lengthened into hours the Quills, staring at the chink in the curtain which proclaimed to the world the inviolability of their home, grew farther and farther apart. Sybil was convinced that something sinister had happened to Caroline. Mr Quill was confirmed in his belief that she had not been in the house with Philip, and could not therefore have received her mother's message.

He looked at his wife out of the corner of his eye, squeezing his lids together so that he could see her better. Although he did not know Sybil's exact age, he was not entirely ignorant of the facts of life. There was, he knew, a period in a woman's life, which he imagined Sybil must have now reached, when she began to think and act peculiarly. His knowledge of the change of life, like his knowledge of all other aspects of the physical lives of men and women, had been picked up through loose and furtive talk at school, in the office, in bars. It would not have surprised Mr Quill, so inaccurate were his opinions on this matter, if Sybil had sprouted a beard and asked for raw beef for breakfast.

Nevertheless, such is the power of silence between two human beings he jumped in his chair when he heard the front door open, and the sound of Caroline's footsteps in the hall. Sybil seemed glued to her chair, staring at the door with frightened eyes. It was Mr Quill who went to meet his daughter. This he did with his usual dignity and balance; having entirely convinced himself that she was innocent.

'Where were you, Caroline?' he asked mildly.

Caroline turned at the bottom of the stairs and looked at her father.

'At the tennis-club,' she said with a smile.

'It's very late. Your mother and I were worried.'

'We had a bit of a dance. I'm sorry I'm late.'

Who were you with at the tennis-club, Caroline?' her father asked with an answering smile. He had always been right about his daughter; he was right now. It seemed to him that there was a very close bond between them; closer than between Caroline and her mother.

'With Mina and Florrie Richardson. Why? Was somebody looking for me?' Caroline had inherited something of her father's talent for the little jarring touch that makes the lie seem so much more probable than truth. At that moment Mr Quill was proud of his daughter for all the wrong reasons.

'No. Your mother and I were just worried about you. You shouldn't stay out so late Carry.'

'Oh, there won't be another dance for ages. Well, I'd better go to bed. Good night, Daddy. Good night, Mammy.'

Mr Quill turned back to his wife with a smile.

'If there's one thing you can always tell on a child's face,' he said, 'it's the truth.'

18

'YOU are,' said Lilian, 'the most unmitigated bitch I have ever met.'

'Yes, dear,' said Rose, 'I know. Everybody says so.'

'This thing would have ended in the usual way, the same as all the others. There was no point in dragging her poor parents into it, except out of sheer malice.'

'It will do them good,' said Rose comfortably. 'They live in a cloud-cuckoo-land of their own making, like these peasant politicians that run this country now, except that the politicians don't believe their own nonsense. The Quills do. A little bit of the truth now and again is the best thing that could happen to them. Besides it was for the child's own good.'

'A lot you care for her good,' said Lilian, stubbing out her cigarette on the cracked saucer which Rose used as an ashtray, and which was placed on a chair set between them on the hearth-rug in place of a table. Like those people who do not admit to drinking by keeping no glasses in the house, Rose, who smoked like a furnace, never admitted it to anybody; and, to prove it, provided no proper ashtrays for herself or her visitors.

Now she heaved herself up out of her armchair and stood over the younger woman, looking greedily at the open packet of cigarettes which lay on the chair beside the saucer.

'Oh, help yourself, you old fraud,' said Lilian, taking up the packet and handing it to her. 'I know you love it.'

'I don't.' The old woman lit up and blew smoke defiantly over her guest's head. 'I only smoke to keep people company.'

'You mean you only smoke other people's cigarettes.'

Rose chuckled fatly and waddled back to her chair, which creaked under her weight like a rusty gate.

'You are enjoying yourself, aren't you dear?' She tapped ash on to the dirty carpet, on which the sun shone like a stream of water poured over a muddy pavement.

'Enjoying myself!' Lilian drew in her breath so quickly that she choked, and doubled over in a fit of coughing. When she straightened she looked at Rose with streaming eyes.

'You're smoking too many cigarettes,' said Rose calmly. 'But just at the moment you're enjoying yourself. You only fling comfortable insults like that at an old friend who's pleased you, even if you don't want to admit it.'

Lilian wiped her eyes with her handkerchief and fingered her neck gently.

'If you mean—'

'I mean that you're really delighted that I told the Quills about their daughter and Philip. You're getting a little tired of being an understanding wife. Everybody does at some time or another. Besides you're afraid of this one. It wasn't like the others, was it? Bringing her to Jim's house for one thing. Or perhaps it's just that Philip is getting older. And so my dear are you.'

Lilian stared at her with hostile eyes for a few moments, while Rose stared back, blinking a little and smiling, as she held her cigarette poised before her mouth. Then the younger woman got up and went over to the open glass door.

'That's the worst of you old witches,' she said quietly. 'You hit on a little bit of truth that amazes people, and if they're foolish enough they imagine that you've read their souls. You should have been a fortune-teller, Rose. You'd have been a great success.'

'It isn't too late to start dear. I'm a great one for turning over a new leaf.'

Lilian tapped on the blistered window-post with her fingernail.

'Yes, of course I'm afraid, if you want to know. But not so much of her. There's no future in that sort of thing for a young girl like that. She'll get over it. I'm afraid for myself.'

'Aren't we all, dear.'

'Yes, you were right there. I am getting older and more tired. I've put up with these little affairs—' she stopped herself, and gripped her elbows in the palms of her hands. Desperately as she wanted to talk to somebody, she knew that Rose could not be trusted. Nothing would delight the old woman more than to hear that Lilian was no longer sure that she loved her husband. It was the sort of thing she specialized in. How many broken romances had the old spinster helped along, gently picking the pieces apart; until at the end one found oneself alone with her staring at the empty future? Already, thought Lilian, she has helped me along the same path, for the simple reason that I was half-prepared to go. She shivered as she turned back to face the fusty room.

'Now you're no longer sure that you love him any more, isn't that it dear?'

'No, Rose, you're quite wrong,' said Lilian in a firm voice. 'I'm thinking of the two boys.'

'The two boys?' Rose was taken unawares by this sudden change of emphasis. Then she blinked and recovered herself. 'You mean young Philip and Tom. Aren't they in Winchester with your mother?'

'They're coming back next week.'

'Well, what has that to do with it?' Rose never wasted time talking about children, except to profess on occasion how much she adored them. Like all complete egoists her preoccupation was with the adult world.

Lilian, more sure of herself, came back to the fireplace and lit another cigarette, leaving the packet back on the arm of Rose's chair.

'It has a lot to do with it. Philip is twelve now and Tom eleven. Children sense things, you know. Very soon Phil is going to notice things about his father, perhaps even to pick up things at school. I don't want that to happen.'

'Well then dear, I was perfectly right to warn the Quills about what was going on.' Rose lifted her shoulders and chuckled, allowing her massive head to sink into the folds of her neck.

'You were perfectly wrong,' said Lilian coldly. 'You know as well as I do that this thing is still going on. He's still meeting her at Uncle Jim's house. I don't know what her parents have done. I suppose she's lied her way out of it. They seem to me to be the sort of couple who would be easy to deal with in that way. What you have done is to make the whole thing more furtive and more desperate than it is. Since it happened Philip has become even more remote and preoccupied than he used to be. Defiant too.

You know how he can't bear to be interfered with. If you had left things as they were the whole thing would have blown over—'

'And then there would have been somebody else.' Rose helped herself to another cigarette and lit it from the stub of the old. She coughed chestily and thumped her vast bosom with her fist. 'No, dear, you're just about tired of the whole thing, aren't you? It isn't simply the children, is it?' She looked at the other woman with narrowed eyes through the cigarette smoke; and felt a surge of pleasure at Lilian's obvious distress.

Lilian sat down on the arm of her chair and looked over Rose's head at the glass front of the bookcase, behind which the rows of Victorian classics reposed: remote, undusted, unread: ghostly behind the thick panes over which the sunlight danced and flickered like water reflected on the ceiling of a house by the sea. She was thinking of how for the first time in her life she was being dishonest with the old woman. Is this how it begins, she wondered? Can the empty, the burnt-out ever be honest?

'By the way,' she asked in the flat voice people use for social questions that need no thought, 'does Mrs Quill still come to visit you'?

'Of course. She didn't for a few days after I told her. But she drifted back. I suppose she's got used to me or something. She never talks about it though, which tells me a lot. The girl may have succeeded in fooling her father, but it's not so easy to pull the wool over a mother's eyes, no matter how harmless she may be. Even if Sybil had stuck her head in the sand for the moment she isn't really fooled. Oh, she knows all right. If she thought I'd told her a lie she'd never have come back. I notice she keeps on watching me in a way she never used to. I expect she wants me to come across with some more information.' Rose chuckled deeply, clamped her cigarette between her lips and beat her huge thighs playfully with her fists. 'And I will too in my own good time. About her husband.'

Lilian sprang to her feet. This time she was really angry.

'You evil old bitch,' she exclaimed, throwing her cigarette half-smoked into the empty fireplace.

'What polite expressions they taught you at Winchester to be sure,' said Rose delightedly. 'And when I was young we used to be told how refined the English were supposed to be. Another illusion gone.'

'If you do this I'll never talk to you again, Rose. I mean that.' Lilian picked up her car-keys from the chair and rattled them angrily on her forefinger.

'Oh, yes you will, dear. After this silly little affair there will be another, and then another and another. And you'll want to find out who it is, and old Rose will tell you. Except of course you lose interest in him completely so that you don't care who he's sleeping with. Perhaps he'll take to the boys. I often wondered why Philip didn't, so many Irish men are that way. It's such a relief to wives. Then you won't care any more. You'll come and gossip, just like all the others. It passes the time, dear. We all come to it sooner or later. Gossip for the women, whiskey for the men.'

Lilian's anger had grown cold. She looked down at the old woman. Like all malicious people Rose had always enjoyed a certain immunity. Others were either afraid of her, or secure in their own good nature, amused and unwilling to really hurt her. There is always something defenceless about those who make it their life's business to hurt others: they are like spoiled children screaming in the dark, and are rarely punished. Now when Lilian spoke she was not so much attacking Rose as fighting something which she recognized in herself.

'What an empty life you must have, Rose,' she said quietly. 'Was it your own fault, or did you let it get you down ? Well, much as it would please you I don't intend to let that happen to me, or to Philip either. I'm not going to live the rest of my days eating my heart out alone. I'm not going to allow myself to get bitter. Of course I'm jealous, if you want to know. Of course I'm hurt. But it's better than to be unable to feel anything at all.'

Lilian stopped, overcome with confusion and doubt. Rose had taken the attack better than she had expected. She was looking at her with a curious expression, half-tender, half-mocking.

'I know dear, I know,' she said soothingly. 'I'm always here if you want me.'

19

'I HAVE only half an hour,' said Caroline.

'It's not enough.' Philip touched her cheek lightly. Her skin was like sun-warmed marble under his cold fingertips.

'They watch me all the time now, I mean my mother does.' Caroline turned her head away and looked across the drawing-room to where the holland blinds drawn against the sun glowed with a faded yellow radiance. Beyond was the garden she knew so well, and below the great blue-green bay. It was like looking at a canvas from which a well-loved picture has been erased; a picture which one can reconstruct in every detail in one's mind.

'She doesn't believe you of course.'

'No. She wants to, but she doesn't, really.'

'And your father?' Philip's voice was light.

'Oh, he believes me all right.'

He took her hand and attempted to draw her to him; but she shook her head and moved away. In the honey-dark twilight of the room her face was shadowed and drawn.

'If you kiss me I won't be able to go.'

'Half an hour is worse than not meeting at all,' he said, raising his voice with sudden passion. The briefness of their recent meetings; the awareness that the world outside, which had once seemed so vague and careless, was now clear-cut and watchful, had sharpened his desire, and increased his need for the blind release of love-making. He was like a man facing bankruptcy who goes on spending more recklessly than ever.

'No, it isn't, Philip. It means we're keeping in touch. It's better than not to meet.'

He was silent.

'It's a terrible thing to be watched.' She put her hand on the mantelpiece and leaned her forehead upon it. The marble was as cold under her palm as his fingers; but it warmed under her flesh. Her voice when she spoke had a hollow echo as it resounded from the empty fireplace. 'I've never known it before. I read a book about a prison once. They have a spy-hole in the door and the jailer may look in at any time. It's like that.'

He came and stood beside her, staring at her bent head in the mirror.

'If only they'd say something,' she burst out. 'Instead of keeping up this pretence that nothing is happening. I never liked rows. I remember at school how terrified I used to be when some of the other girls told us of the awful fights their parents used to have. But it's better that than this. I know that now. Finding Mammy watching me out of the window whenever I go out. Listening to Daddy trying to make jokes.'

'I thought you said your father believed you.' He put his elbows on the mantelpiece, supporting his temples with his fist, and stared at his own dim ivory face in the glass. It stared back at him like a painting of someone long dead that one had once known well. The long years of casual pretence with Lilian had taken their toll. It was difficult for him now to be less than watchful with anybody. He was unable to cut through, with a gesture, a look, an inflexion of the body, to the unspoken things that lovers understand with their blood. Resisting the love he no

124

longer wanted from his wife, he had given up his freedom of action.

'You can believe and not believe,' she said without raising her head. 'Daddy is like that.'

'You have grown up,' he said softly to her in the mirror.

'I never knew how difficult it is to hurt anybody in cold blood. I don't think I ever knew what it was really like to have a father and mother before. It's easy to say I'm going to walk out on them, get away from it all, but I can't, Philip. I can't. And they're going to destroy us, I know they are. If only they'd attack me or something. Accuse me of all the things people are supposed to accuse you of when you've done something like I've done—then it would be easy. I could take a room somewhere, and we could be together whenever we want to. But they don't. They don't say anything, and I can't say anything. We're all dumb.'

'Silence is a great deal more terrifying than speech,' said Philip, touching her shoulder. But she drew away from him along the length of the great carved fireplace, finding some small relief in cooling her palm on another part of the cold marble.

'Don't touch me,' she whispered. 'Don't touch me Philip, please. I can't bear that either. I can't bear anybody to touch me now, even in the 'bus or in the church. I want to be by myself all the time, except when I'm with you, and I don't want you to touch me any more.'

The chains of love by which they were both tied—he to a faithful wife, she to her bewildered parents—had tightened and were drawing them apart. The love that is most powerful and terrifying of all: love that is carried in the blood and stored in the bones; love that is ruthless and unending in a way that passion can never be; love that throws a light from its merciless flame, beyond which all is darkness and doubt. Even the boldest only explore its rim, one foot in the shadows, the other in the ancestral glow. Caroline, who would have been capable a few months ago of following her lover to the ends of the earth, now knew with the sure knowledge of the body that she was not loved as she had wanted to be. It was her body that rebelled against his touch: her body that knew, carrying in it as it did the seeds of the past and the shadow of the future.

It was this body, which in the past few months had ripened and matured into the body of a woman, that now excited Philip to a tenderness that he had known only once before. To young lovers imprisoned in the golden radiance of their first desire there is infinite tenderness in the first touching of hands, the awkward kiss, the clumsy embrace. To the older, the experienced, the mismatched, it comes often at the end of love, as a vision of childhood is said to flit across the fading eyesight of a dying man. Those who part in anger never really part at all.

'Please,' he begged, reaching out again to touch her. But she lifted her head, her hands pressed palms outward against her breasts, and faced him.

'No.'

'We have only a few minutes left. Let me kiss you.'

'No. No.' She turned quickly and hurried from the room. For a moment, as she paused in the dark hall, she had the same sensation of terror as that which had assailed her on the first evening she had come to the house, when Philip had left her alone in the drawing-room. She looked up the shadowy stairs which ended now in night. Then she ran to the door and began to fumble with the lock, which was old and stiff and had always given her trouble. Before she could open it Philip was by her side, holding her hands tightly in his own.

'Don't go,' he whispered. 'Please don't go.'

She leaned her shoulder against the door and groaned as his hands relinquished hers and closed gently about her neck. She threw back her head and stared at the ceiling. The sun rippling through the trees outside threw a patch from the fanlight that wavered and flowed like a reflection of water. The same illusion that Lilian had had a few days before as she looked over Rose Blake's head at the light dancing on the glass of the bookcase.

'No, no,' she said weakly as she felt his mouth on her throat. Then she cried out in pain and terror as his hands cupped her breasts. She tore herself away from him and fell back against the door, covering her breasts with her crossed arms.

'What is it, Caroline? What's the matter? What have I done?' So strong was his desire that he could not believe that it would not be indulged.

'I must go, Philip. I must. I told them I'd be back in half an hour.'

'It isn't that. You'd have stayed if I hadn't touched you, wouldn't you?'

'I must go.' Her hand fumbling with the lock had unfastened the clasp. She swung the big door open and ran out on to the avenue. But he was too quick for her. Before she could get past the car parked at the bottom of the steps he had caught up with her, and was holding her fast by the arm.

'Caroline, it isn't your parents, it isn't any of that at all. What is it?'

'Philip, please let me go,' she said weakly. 'I don't feel well this evening. I—'

'You don't feel well,' he repeated, looking at her slightly swollen face, at the circles under her eyes, at the dark patch on her forehead. 'Caroline, is it—?'

'No, no,' she cried, staring at him with frightened eyes, her lips trembling as if she had been struck. 'I'm all right. Let me go. It takes me about twenty minutes to walk if I don't get a 'bus. I'm late already. I said I was going to the church.'

'Then I will leave you at the church. I'm not going to let you walk. Come.' He opened the door of the car and made her get in, holding her shoulder gently but firmly. He turned the car and moved off down the avenue, the gravel crunching like pounded rice under the wheels. They went back the same way they had come the first evening. But she did not look at the bay, swaying beneath its golden-blue palisade of mountains. Huddled in the corner of her seat, with her hands clasped so tightly that the knuckles shone, she was as remote as Philip had been on that first evening. She had learned the lesson of silence.

The Mercedes drew up by the kerb on the far side of the church. Sybil, lingering in the porch, uncertain of what to do now that she knew her daughter was not inside, saw it, and drew back into the shadows. Her face under its torn black mantilla was yellow and frightened. She knew the car, recognized Caroline, and saw Philip's profile outlined against the far window. They sat quite still for a few minutes; minutes that seemed an eternity to Sybil. She was no longer aware of the soft swish of the baize door behind her, the little click of the confessional slats, the shuffling of feet on the stone steps. She was watching the car as intently as Caroline on another evening, when she had waited where her mother was standing now for its arrival. An evening as rose-tinted, languorous, and heavy-laden with the scents of summer as this one. The sun shone heedless and magnificent; the beech trees in the gardens opposite threw down their dappled shade over the car; the dust lay warm as bleached sand on the road. Nothing had changed about the strident, new red-brick church: nothing would ever change within it, except the ageing faces of the men and women who passed silently through its porch. A girl waiting for her lover; a mother racked by doubts; a coffin followed by a straggle of mourners; a nurse carrying a wool-wrapped bundle to the baptistry; an old woman climbing the steps painfully one by one; a bride in white lace descending them: it was all one here. Old stories that had been told many times before; and would be repeated again under the winking eye of the sanctuary lamp.

Sybil drew into the sheltering gloom as she saw her daughter get out of the car, and cross the street towards the church. In a sudden panic she turned, drawing her mantilla about her face, and pretended to read the notices pinned upon the wall. But Caroline did not see her as she passed with bowed head, over which she had placed a small white handkerchief, into the church. When Sybil turned round the car had disappeared, as silently as it came, leaving only a trail of diamond-shaped tyre-marks in the dust; tracks that were soon obliterated by the passing traffic.

She went down the steps and turned towards home; knowing now that Caroline would be back in a short while: knowing also what the future held in store, and what she must do.

20

THE O'Connor boys were four days late in coming home. They had been delayed because their grandmother had tripped over one of her chihuahuas in the garden and sprained her ankle. Lilian and Philip went to the airport to meet them. They were met on arrival with the announcement that the flight would be ten minutes late.

'We should have known,' muttered Philip darkly, as they went upstairs to the bar for a drink. 'It'll probably be an hour late. They always are.'

'Oh, don't say that Philip,' said Lilian. 'It's the first time they've flown and I'm worried. I'll have a Martini.'

'Not a cloud in the sky,' said Philip, coming back with the drinks, 'and they have to be late.'

'We should have sent them by boat.' Lilian gazed out over the silver runways to the flat green fields beyond. 'But they wanted so much to fly. Phil of course will be all right, but I hope Tom doesn't get nervous and be sick or something.'

'Of course he won't,' said Philip, raising his hand in greeting to a business acquaintance, who was acquiring Dutch courage at the counter with an enormous whiskey and soda.

'And then that long train journey up from Winchester, they'll be exhausted.'

'Nonsense, Lilian. At their age they'll love it. You've just got to make up your mind that the train was probably late, and the 'plane will be late. Nothing ever runs on time now.'

'I hate postponements,' said Lilian querulously, tapping her glass with her cocktail stick. 'It was ridiculous of Mummy to change the flight, and keep them four days longer just because she sprained her foot. Oh, Lord, there goes that loudspeaker again.'

She lifted her head to listen with a frown of concentration; but all that could be heard across the public address system was a violent crackling, behind which a blurred voice muttered something inaudible.

'The age of efficiency?' said Philip, not without a certain grim satisfaction, as he went across to the barman to ask him to telephone down for information. The barman told him there was a telephone through the dining-room and down the passage. The business acquaintance threw a heavy arm about his shoulder, and invited him to have a drink before he departed for Amsterdam. Philip excused himself politely.

'Hate flying,' said the man sadly as he turned back and ordered himself another whiskey. 'Don't know why I do it.'

'What did he say?' asked Lilian anxiously.

'He said he hates flying,' said Philip with a grin. 'I don't blame him.'

'The barman?' Lilian's eyebrows shot up.

'No, he told me where the telephone was. I suppose that means it's not his job to 'phone down enquiring for 'planes that don't show up.'

Lilian finished her Martini and stood up.

'We may as well go down to the office and enquire ourselves,' she said.

When they got to the office a long queue separated them from the information desk: people asking about delayed 'planes, about relatives who had not arrived, about the weather in Zurich and Dusseldorf, about the certainty of catching a 'plane connection in Rome within the ten minutes allowed by the travel agency schedule, about a car to Dublin and Killarney, about a bottle of scent left on the 'plane from Paris. In the great glass cage of the entrance hall people scurried about with the tightened expressions of those who have temporarily given up their freedom, and yielded to the impersonal tyranny of a timetable which they have been conditioned to believe in as if it were Holy Writ. Anxious, harried, strained people whose quick nervous footfalls were muffled by the thick rubber flooring. The place, like the lounges of all airports, had the air of a waiting-room in some huge surgical hospital. The ground staff had the impersonal stare and the marshmallow complexions of medical orderlies. From the tarmac beyond the glass doors could be heard the muffled scream of giant engines.

When they got to the information desk the girl informed them, in the accent of international refinement adopted by airport officials, that the flight had already landed. They rushed out of the building and across to the arrivals terminal. Having exchanged an over-enthusiastic wave with the boys as they waited for inspection in the customs hall, Lilian sank on to a bench and closed her eyes with relief.

'They look all right,' said Philip.

'Yes, Phil does, but Tom is ashen. I'll never send them by 'plane again. It isn't worth it. God, I could do with another Martini.'

Philip sat down beside her and leaned forward looking at the floor, holding his clasped hands between his knees.

Lilian got out her lipstick and compact and began to make up her face. When she had finished she stared at the tiny looking-glass, her fingers pressed against her temples.

'I look like death. One doesn't want to give the boys the impression that one is frightened,' she said, snapping the compact shut and putting it back into her bag.

'Here they come,' said Philip.

Lilian jumped up and hurried across the hall to greet her sons. She was always meticulous in her formalities. Tom was always greeted with a shade less exuberance than his elder brother, because Lilian had long ago admitted to herself that Tom was her favourite. With his Victorian good looks, his pale oval face, huge dark eyes and blue-black hair, he reminded her of her father who had died when she was twenty. Philip, red-haired, snub-nosed, freckled and uncomplicated, was a remote throwback to his father's people. Now he looked guiltily about him as his mother embraced Tom; an embrace that was less brief than usual, since the boy was trembling, and had clung to her as she kissed him and smoothed back the raven lock which fell over his forehead.

'All right, Tom?' she said gently.

The boy nodded and shook hands gravely with his father. Phil, disengaging himself hastily from his mother's arms, squared his shoulders and greeted his father's hand-clasp with a gruff and manly nod. As there were no porters to be seen the two boys picked up their cases and followed their parents to the car.

'Did you have a good flight?' said Lilian as they moved off.

'Terrific,' said Phil enthusiastically. 'One air-pocket after another. Half the passengers were sick, and one old lady started to cry. The pilot had to come out to her. I'd love to be a pilot.'

'How is Granny?' went on Lilian, unable to repress a shudder as she thought of Tom glued to his seat in the wind-tossed 'plane.

'She saw us off at the train,' said Tom, holding up a slim square parcel he was carrying. 'And she bought me this record in Mrs Freeman's shop in the High Street.'

'Good heavens,' said Lilian, who always grew absent-minded when she was upset, 'is old Mrs Freeman still alive? We used to buy Galli-Curci records from her when I was a girl.'

'It's Miss Freeman who runs the place now,' said Phil, putting her right. 'Granny says she's an old maid.'

Lilian and Philip laughed, and speaking at the same time, asked Tom what record his grandmother had bought him. Lilian broke off in the middle of the question and allowed her husband to finish it. She looked down at her hands clasped on her lap, and gently moved her wedding ring with her thumb. She found tears smarting her eyes. The shared thought had moved her by its complete unexpectedness. In earlier days she would have taken it happily for granted.

'The Mozart Clarinet Concerto,' said Tom proudly. 'They hadn't it in stock, so it had to be ordered from London. Please may I play it when I get home?'

'Of course, Tom,' said Philip. 'And did Granny buy anything for you, Phil?'

'A Meccano set. Miss Freeman had to order that from London too.'

'Good heavens, not another one,' said Philip with a side-long look at his wife.

'This one is atomic,' said Phil reprovingly. 'The very latest.'

Lilian pulled down the sunshade in front of her and looked at the boys in the mirror at the back. Tom was looking out at the brilliant green fields, an affectionate half smile playing about his full mouth. Phil was leaning forward with screwed-up eyes, eagerly watching the oncoming traffic, and darting triumphant glances at the cars they passed.

'It's very calm down here,' he said disapprovingly. 'No high winds at all. Isn't it funny?'

'We've had a heat-wave for ages,' said Lilian. 'Lovely weather. Didn't you have the same in Winchester? Granny said in her letters that the weather was very good.'

'Not as good as here,' said Tom, staring out with dreamy eyes at the blue mountains encircling Dublin. Lilian, following his glance over the jumbled roof-tops into the shadow of which they were descending, felt a sudden pang of nostalgia for the blood-red walls, the ancient echoing lanes, the old royal patina of her native city. She thought sadly that she would never really belong to the country her favourite son was returning to with such affection in his eyes.

'Well,' she asked briskly, 'how did you like Winchester?'

'It's terrible old,' said Phil promptly. 'Nothing but tea-shops, and everybody talking in whispers. But,' he went on, jumping up and down on his seat with excitement, 'Granny brought us to Southampton one day. That was terrific. I never saw so many ships, and it's lovely and noisy. It must be great to be a captain, except that it's better to be an air-pilot. If you ask me ships are a thing of the past.'

'Did you like Winchester Tom?' asked his father.

'Oh, yes. Granny brought us to the Cathedral—'

'Nothing but tombs,' snorted Phil.

'Oh, but Jane Austen is buried there,' protested Lilian loyally.

'I saw that,' said Tom eagerly. 'And the house where she died. And Granny took us to the God Begot, which she says is the oldest inn in England, and to St Catherine's Hill, and William the Conqueror's Palace—'

'Nothing but a few old stones,' said Phil disgustedly.

'And the Buttercross, and the *Hampshire Chronicle* office, and King Arthur's statue, and where the Dominican monastery used to be. Imagine a Dominican monastery in England!'

'What did you like best, Tom?' asked Lilian with a smile.

'Minster Street and the Square,' he answered promptly. 'Why?'

'I don't know. I think because it reminded me of home. It's a little bit like Fitzwilliam Square.'

Lilian was silent; and again felt a ridiculous flush of tears.

'Granny has pups,' said Phil, anxious to get off the boring subject of antiquities; and banishing, as he invariably did, the slightest suggestion of tension. Phil was an invaluable arbitrator in any company. Lilian had more than once been indebted to him for his sublime lack of nerves, and wished very much that she could love him as much as his brother who, moody, sensitive, demanding affection, would one day she knew hurt her very much.

Philip laughed.

'What, more of them!'

'This is the best litter she ever had. One of the puppies is so small it's like a mouse, and Granny says it'll only be a pound weight when it grows up, and she'll make it into a champion. And the others she's going to sell at forty guineas each. Oh, boy!'

'Oh, I forgot,' said Tom eagerly, 'how are Muff and Tubby? Why didn't you bring them with you?'

'Well, they don't really care for dogs in public places like airports, darling. They're very well. Muff has been a little overcome with the heat, and I've kept her in a good deal, but Tubby doesn't seem to mind.'

'It won't be long until we're home now,' said Tom, pressing his nose to the glass of the window and staring out at the brutal Victorian façades of Northumberland Road. Philip, glancing at the traffic in the driving mirror, caught sight of his son with flatted nose and whitened forehead, like a child at a sweet-shop window, and suffered one of those moments of confusion when we recognize a gesture, a word, a posture out of the past, with our bodies but not with our minds. He jerked the steering wheel violently to the right, narrowly avoiding a 'bus in front as he shot out alongside it. To get through the lane of on-coming traffic he had to press down hard on the accelerator, leaning forward over the wheel with strained white knuckles. But the big car responded silently and ruth-lessly, shooting out in front of the 'bus. Lilian, with a quick glance at her husband's strained profile, sank back on her seat with a sigh of relief.

'Twelve minutes from here, if we go on at this rate,' said Phil, looking at his watch with delight. As if responding to some challenge from his elder son Philip kept on driving at the same reckless speed. Lilian glanced round quickly at the boys in the back. Phil was leaning forward excitedly, willing the car to still greater speed with little spasmodic jerks of his body. Tom had turned back from the window and was staring thoughtfully at the back of his father's head.

'Oh, boys,' cried Phil, flinging himself back and looking out of the rear window, 'that's a Jaguar we're after passing. Look at the way that man is looking at us. I bet he's real mad.'

Tom gripped the back of the front seat with his two hands, and, catching his mother's eye in the mirror, looked at her with the same thoughtful expression with which he had examined his father's head. Oh, God, thought Lilian, looking away, what is he thinking? For once Phil's healthy boyish enthusiasm failed to reconcile her to this sudden dangerous speeding. At one time, even a few months ago, she would have spoken sharply to her husband; but now she sat frozen in her seat unable to utter a word. The drive became a nightmare thing. Walls buckled and wavered like corrugated iron. Trees lining the road seemed to bend back with crazy trailing branches, like long hair loosened and whipped by a storm. The path fled past like rushing water; and the inexorable road contracted and rose to meet them with the unrelenting motion of a conveyor belt. Faces behind the windows of cars passed so quickly that they seemed to be stationary, were blurred and devoid of humanity; and the green-topped hill with its slender steeple, in the shadow of which they lived, lurched against the luminous sky as they raced the last few hundred yards to the gates of the house.

With a whoop Phil sprang from the car and opened them; and then began to race like a mad thing up the avenue in front of them. As the car moved forward slowly behind him Tom leaned out and touched his mother's shoulder. Lilian shuddered and clasped her son's hot dry hand. When they drew up before the front door Phil was jumping up and down with excitement.

'We did it in thirty-two minutes, Daddy.' He took off his wrist-watch and waved it over his head. Philip got out of the car and ran up the steps to open the door.

'Come on, Phil,' said Lilian, squeezing his hand and forcing a smile, 'you must be starved.'

The evening to which she had looked forward with such pleasure loomed ominously before her. An evening during which the supper which she had so carefully prepared with the cook would have to be eaten with a show of enthusiasm. An evening in which Philip would indulge that streak of neurotic boisterousness which always frightened her, resembling as it did the sudden change sometimes brought about by drink in the character of a shy and gentle man. A family gathering during which they would have to look at Phil build his Meccano set on the drawing-room floor; and listen to Tom's record. Philip had always spent a lot of his time with his sons; and Lilian knew that he loved them with an oblique tenderness which concealed an immense passion and pride. No matter how difficult things had been, it had always been easy to forget them on an evening such as this. But Lilian knew that it would no longer be easy. So much had always depended on her own ability to forget her fears; even more on Philip's genuine delight in the worship of his two sons. Now she would have to act the part of the happy mother; terrified that some day she would see her younger son watching his father's face with accusing eyes.

21

ALTHOUGH Sybil Quill always succeeded in impressing her relations on her annual visit to the midlands with her knowledge of 'bus-routes, cinemas, and novenas at various Dublin churches, in fact the city had scarcely impinged on her consciousness at all. She remained a provincial; sometimes impressed by the misty beauty of the sea and mountains that encircled the city, and always a little frightened of the traffic. But she had never adjusted herself to the tempo of the place: the quick, Dublin wit seemed to her, when she was aware of it, as unfunny and obscure as Cockney to a native of Clydeside. Bred among the slow-eyed malice, the watchfulness and the complex blood kindness of her native place, she thought the Dubliners slick and superficial; the eternal complaint of the country-woman, whose roots remain deep in heavy soil, against the potted brightness of city flowers.

But when she became aware that disaster had entered her life she made the mistake of investing her adopted home with all the manners of her country town, where those who have sinned against the harsh and narrow laws of the community were never really forgiven, and never forgotten. It seemed to her now, with all the faith that is inspired by a sudden vision of brightness, that the whole of Dublin was watching her and her daughter.

It never occurred to Sybil that Dublin did not care. The affairs of a man like Philip O'Connor were certainly talked about, for he was rich and influential. But it was gossip of an ill-informed and desultory kind, thinning out towards the edges, like the ripples from a stone dropped into a stagnant pool. Dublin, yellow-eyed, ripe of lip and lazy of arm, did not really care. The idle chatter was slothfully malicious, a little envious, and boastful as always, like the talk of a group of actors huddled about a bar-table after a first night they know has not been a success. But there was no hard core of moral indignation; nothing, when the tale was told that whiled away the dipping time, would ever be done. Dublin was used to scandals, real and invented. In the never-ending flow of talk that rose and fell like the Liffey tides, some ligan, thrown overboard to lighten the load for the next intake of human cargo, found its way to the mud-banks; but nobody ever bothered to pick it up. The people who see in Dublin an arbiter of morals really only judge themselves and their own guilt. For Dublin has no morals.

And so, as Sybil watched her daughter, she watched alone. She knew that Caroline had not given up meeting Philip, although she knew that these meetings were very brief. Since she was neither a harsh nor a consistently decisive woman she did not know what to do, except to go on watching, and placate the household gods that she carried with her from her native place. And so every night the light was on in her front parlour, with the curtains drawn an inch apart to throw a beam of certainty upon a heedless world. She had felt like going to Mass every morning; but to do so when it was not her habit would, she knew, in her own town, have prepared the neighbours for imminent calamity. So she took to dropping into the church several times a day to light a candle before the altar of the Sacred Heart, and before the statue of St Joseph, to whom she had a particular devotion, having said a novena to him for a husband before she met Mr Quill. Sybil's faith, although careless and without passion, like that of so many Irish people, was nevertheless strong and deep. It was the faith of the journeyman of God: unemotional, practical, materialistic—when she bought a candle for St Joseph she expected him to do something about it—but in the last resort rigid and completely unshakeable. And so it was no surprise to her at all that one morning, after staying on her knees for hours the night before in the church, matters came to a head between her and her daughter.

Mr Quill had gone out to his car to go to the office, and Sybil and Caroline were left alone. For some weeks now every meal, especially luncheon which they ate together, had been as much an ordeal for the mother as it was for the daughter. Both knew what was on the other's mind. Caroline, bewildered, lost, was unable to speak, since like all the young and happy she had always spoken with her heart, and had not yet learned to speak without it. It is the cold-hearted, the wary, who make passionate speeches: the young in love are dumb. Sybil, remembering in her bones the irrevocable power of speech, had also kept silent; some age-old superstitious awe telling her that what is not said is never brought to light.

The empty breakfast things stood on the table between the two women. A bowl of sugar, in which a brown lump had formed because Mr Quill had taken a last helping with a wet teaspoon; three empty cups, on the sides of which tea-leaves had formed curious little patterns, which Sybil sometimes contemplated thoughtfully, regretting that unlike her mother she had never learned to read them; a half-eaten loaf of bread; a teapot and a chipped spout that leaked; and—another relic of the legacy—a silver milk-jug. Sybil stirred the last grains of sugar in the bottom of her cup with aimless fingers. Suddenly the silence was broken by the sharp clatter of china falling to the ground. Caroline, her eyes heavy with sleeplessness, had started to rise from the table and had dashed her cup to the floor with her elbow. The saucer rolled along the linoleum on its rim and came to rest unharmed under the window; but the cup had hit the corner of the sideboard and lay broken in pieces on the floor. The two women stared at it for what seemed to both of them an age. Then Caroline sank back into her chair, covered her face with her hands and began to weep. Her thin shoulders, pointed and angular under her cotton frock, shuddered as she pressed the balls of her thumbs against her eye-sockets. She made no sound as she acknowledged the end of her summer; a summer which still glittered as brightly and as heedlessly as it had when she first ran to Philip's arms. She used to think that the sun had shone for their love. It shone now, no less burningly, for the end of it.

Sybil got down on her knees and began to gather up the broken bits of china. Then she sat back on her heels, holding the pieces in her lap, and looked up at her daughter.

'Don't cry, Carry. It's only an old cup. It was cracked anyhow.'

Caroline made no reply, but pressed her palms closer against her eyes to prevent the tears from rolling down her cheeks. Sybil got up, clutching the broken pieces in one hand, and supporting herself against the leg of the table with the other. She started for the kitchen, but at the door of the little room she stopped, turned back, and came to her daughter's side. She left the broken china on the table and put her arm about Caroline's shoulder. The girl made no effort to draw away, or to rest her head against her mother's body: she just sat there dumb and frozen.

'I'll make you another cup of tea,' said Sybil. She could think of nothing else to say. But she did not release her daughter; and made no effort to go into the kitchen. Outside with a spluttering roar Mr Quill's car started, and moved off with little staccato grunts. Suddenly Caroline moved, freeing herself from her mother's arms and turning her face away.

'I can't go to the office today, Mammy,' she whispered. 'Will you ring up?'

'Of course I will, Carry. I'll make you another cup of tea.'

'I don't want another cup of tea, Mammy.'

Sybil bent down and took her daughter's chin in her hand, forcing her to turn her head and face her. She saw now in the upturned face, as if magnified by a glass, the things that she had watched secretly for the past few weeks: the dull eyes with their purple circles, the swollen mouth and puffy cheeks, the darkened skin on the forehead. Sybil drew back and hit Caroline hard with her clenched fist.

The girl stared at her mother's shocked face for a moment, and then slowly wiped her wet cheeks with the back of her hand. She made no effort to touch the spot on her neck which her mother had struck; indeed she seemed to be unaware of it. Sybil turned away and sat down heavily on her chair.

'You can't go to the office any more,' she said.

'I don't want to go. I'll have to go away.'

'Yes,' said Sybil pouring herself a half-cup of cold tea. 'Yes, you will.'

'I have some money saved, about twenty pounds. I'll be able to get a job in England.'

'Are you sure?'

'Yes, two of the girls from the office went six months ago, and they wrote several times to me since. They said they could get a job for me. Everybody is going anyway.'

'You'll have to give notice in your office.'

'My holidays are due to me. Oh, I have money to get for them too. That's seven pounds more.'

'What kind of a job is it in England?'

'The same as I have here, an estate agent. Only the money is ten pounds a week there, and I could share a flat with Peggy and Molly.'

'No you won't,' said Sybil sharply. 'Is the job in the same office as they're in?'

'Yes.'

'Then you can't take that either. You'll have to find another job.'

'I didn't think of that.' Caroline looked down at her plate, moistened her forefinger and gathered some crumbs, which she nibbled abstractedly. Her mother sipped her cold tea. The blow, the necessity for which both understood completely, was forgotten. They were two women who could not allow themselves the luxury of recrimination, one because shock had frozen her nerves, the other because she was involved in the dilemma of the flesh of her flesh. So they sat calmly discussing ways and means, money and jobs, the necessity of getting on with life. Humanity indulges in heroics only after the events which, slim, shadowy and often unnoticed, shape their lives.

'It's easy to get a job in England,' said Caroline. 'I know lots of girls who went without one and got themselves fixed up in a few days.'

'Yes, and your shorthand and typing are good. And I suppose they'll give you a good reference at the office.'

'Oh, yes, they will.'

There was nothing more to be said without involving themselves in the emotional scene which they both dreaded. Nothing for Sybil to do except help her daughter to get away as quickly and as silently as possible, as in her home town so many girls had gone away, a little too quickly, a little too brightly: to return in a year or two, harder about the mouth, with watchful eyes and carefully casual manners. It was only necessary that nothing should be said; put into the words that would give shape and substance to a situation that in Sybil's world could never be admitted. She wanted very much now to take her daughter in her arms; to comfort her as women have always comforted one another in their eternal submission to the inexorable laws of their own making.

Although Sybil was a slack and ineffectual woman her instincts derived from a hard school; and now, driven back upon them for the first time since Caroline's birth, she seemed calmer and more decisive than ever before. She accepted without question the fact that her only child must leave her, perhaps never to return; just as Caroline in her own fashion knew the price she would have to pay, and the loneliness she would have to face. Both of them accepted their heritage; a heritage dispensed over long centuries by the people they sprang from: a slow-moving, unforgetting people whose thoughts often seemed moulded by the heavy midland soil that bore them. But these plain-dwellers had never lacked courage, born as they were to the harsh struggle for existence on their purple bog-land, and facing as they did with their opening eyes the great blinding arc of sky, before which no mountains stood as sentinels. Their feet were heavy with turf-mould; but their faces were naked to the heavens.

'Go up to bed, Carry,' said Sybil, getting up with the teapot in her hand. 'I'll ring the office, and make another cup of tea.'

She watched Caroline walk slowly from the room; and then went about her business at the telephone and in the kitchen. Although her movements were mechanical and her heart was heavy, there was at the core of her being an unacknowledged pulse of excitement. There was much to be done; much to be said that Caroline would not hear: but underneath the rage, pity and shame that she felt, there was that instinctive response to life that is the secret of every woman's endurance. Life had stirred again under her roof. And although Sybil believed it to be a shameful life, the stigma of which she and her daughter would bear all their lives, she also knew that it had to be protected.

22

MR QUILL arrived home that night very late to find his wife waiting up for him. He was preparing to go up quietly to bed, having drunk more than his quota of Miss Lee's whiskey, when he heard Sybil calling him from the sitting-room. He steadied himself, shook his head, and walked carefully into the room.

'How is it that you didn't come home for your tea?' asked Sybil sharply. She had been on the point of ringing up Mick's several times during the evening when her husband failed to come home; but once again her ancestral cunning had prompted her course. To summon him back once from his accustomed haunts was admissible; to do it twice within a fortnight might have caused comment. It certainly would have done so in her home town, where pubs were sacred places dedicated to the male idea, from which a man was called from his own kind only in the extremity of death, accident or fire. And so she waited; all the primitive desire for revenge which she had concealed from her daughter mounting within her as she sat alone in the brightly lit sitting-room.

'Ah,' said Mr Quill shaking his head ruefully, and sitting down on a small chair which wobbled under his weight, 'I had a few over the eight with Paul as I was coming out. It's his birthday. Sixty years old today. Would you ever believe it?'

Sybil was not entirely displeased that her husband had put himself in the wrong on this particular night; for she had already convinced herself that he was entirely to blame for the whole affair. Philip O'Connor was his friend not hers. The deep and delicate tenderness which she had displayed towards her daughter was one side of her nature, part of the natural dignity and tact that her mother would have shown in the same circumstances. But social indignation was also part of her world, less deep and searching than the sympathy she felt for Caroline in her age-old pain, yet no less a part of her scheme of things. And it was an indignation that could be shared with the men, as so much else could never be.

'Oh, yes that's right, stay out all night drinking and boozing and leave your wife and child to wait for you alone, without a helping hand or a kind word in their trouble.' Tears of rage and self-pity filled Sybil's faded eyes, and she tugged the bodice of her dress violently into place over her stomach, where it had become crinkled as she sat in her chair hour after hour.

'Is Caroline in?' said Mr Quill innocently, hoping to ward off the storm that hovered over his own head.

Sybil stood up, and going over to the window pulled the curtains together. For what she had to say it was necessary to seal up the chink of light on the outside world.

'Yes, your daughter is in. In bed, where she has been all day. She won't be seeing your friend Philip O'Connor again.'

'Oh, are you at that again. It's a wonder you wouldn't leave that alone.'

'Leave it alone, leave it alone! Is that what you say?' Sybil's voice rose and cracked with rage. She stood poised like an adder in the middle of the room, facing her husband, her thin body bent towards him, her palms pressed against her thighs. 'Do you know that your daughter is in trouble and that Philip O'Connor is the man?'

Although Mr Quill understood the euphemism, which had only one meaning in his vocabulary, he was slow to capture its meaning. Not only because it was impossible; but also because it struck at the very centre of his being: his belief in himself. Half-drunk he stared at his wife as if she had suddenly begun to speak in a foreign language.

'What are you saying?' he said stupidly.

'I'm telling you that your daughter is going to have a baby, and that your friend Philip O'Connor is the father, that's what I'm telling you.' Sybil's voice rose to a hysterical scream. She straightened herself and clutched at her stomach, swaying a little from side to side, as if she were trying to ease a sudden and terrible pain.

Mr Quill lumbered to his feet. He felt that his wife had passed the bounds of decency, and that it was time for him to do something about it.

'Are you gone mad?' he said in a thick voice, swaying a little also like his wife. The tiny room, furnished with so many relics of the legacy, crumpled and swayed about them; but for entirely different reasons.

'I am not gone mad. It's only that I have more interest in your daughter than you have, drinking and boozing and sucking up to Phil O'Connor.' Sybil paused for breath and looked at her handsome husband with something like contempt. For years she had trusted his every word out of the tolerance of indifference; had lived with him casually in the day-to-day intimacy of simple provident living: but now she suddenly saw him as a creature who must be infused with her own vicarious desire for blood.

'Have you no eyes, or no heart, or no feelings at all, John Quill? Can't you see what has happened to your daughter under your own roof? My roof! Something that'll cause us to hang down our heads in shame for the rest of our lives. Oh, God, what have I ever done to deserve such a thing to happen to me!' She stopped and looked up at the ceiling, and then lowered her voice. 'All right, go up and see her, and ask her. Go up and ask your daughter and she'll tell you.'

Something in his wife's tone and manner sobered Mr Quill, and he sat down again and rested his forehead on his hand, hunching his great shoulders as if warding off a blow.

'Well, what are you going to do? Are you going to let that blackguard get away with it? Ruin your only child and go scot-free? Is that what you're going to do, is it?'

Mr Quill was silent. As Sybil had followed the course that she knew her mother would have taken; so now Mr

Quill thought of what his father would have done in the same circumstances. But in his red-brick exile in Dublin; befuddled, confused and miserable, he could not imagine what his father would have done. Such a thing could not possibly have happened in that small tidy home, so far away and so long ago: it was quite inconceivable. Mr Quill had been ill-prepared for life by his parents: they had been too happy.

'Well, what are you going to do?' demanded Sybil inexorably.

'What do you want me to do?' said Mr Quill wearily.

'What do I want you to do!' Sybil's voice rose again. 'What kind of a man are you to ask a question like that? I want you to go and face your friend Philip O'Connor and tell him what has happened, and ask him what he's going to do about it. That's what I want you to do.'

Mr Quill took out his handkerchief and mopped his sweating brow. And while he was doing it he thought of the seventy pounds he owed Philip and the ten pounds he owed Miss Lee, and all the bills that had somehow to be paid out of the next cheque. He turned in his chair and looked at his wife, rolling his handkerchief between his wet palms.

'I can't go to Philip, Sybil. I owe him money.'

'Well, pay him back. Get the money and go up to him and throw it in his face. And if you're half a man you'll give him the thrashing he deserves.'

'But we have no money Sybil,' said Mr Quill simply. 'I can't pay him back.'

'No money! What do you mean no money! Haven't you your cheque coming in at the end of the month?'

'Yes I have, and I also have two solicitors' letters from Murphy the grocer, and Maguire the butcher for the bills we owe them. That's why I borrowed the money from Philip in the first place. And there are other bills too. We're up to our necks in debt. We can't afford to do anything.'

Husband and wife stared at each other for a long time,

and although Mr Quill had not his spectacles on, Sybil was standing near enough for him to see the blank amazement in her eyes; an expression that was followed by one of total incomprehension. Then she turned away and sat down on her chair, plucking at the skirt of her dress. Twenty years of self-deception dies hard; and Sybil at that moment, with her red velvet curtains drawn against a darkening sky, was as yet unaware that her harmless, improvident and altogether unimportant little world had collapsed about her feet. She was no longer an heiress, with a handsome husband, and a pretty daughter, who could afford to sit in the best seats at the cinemas and disregard the winter sales. She was a frightened middle-aged woman who suddenly and unwillingly had been made to realize the harsh reality on which even the most sheltered existence is founded. Money had enabled her to build the little dream-world in which she had existed aimlessly for so long; and now at the end of it it was money that shattered it. The gods we create exact their tribute out of the clay in which we mould them. Although it was warm in the overfurnished little room Sybil shivered. Her body rather than her mind, which was numb, was acknowledging the cold bare truth that so few have the courage to discover for themselves: that love dies, dreams fade, and that we are all in those stark moments of our lives, when we stand naked before the dagger of truth, alone.

Mr Quill, sitting disconsolately opposite his wife, was not shivering. He was a man slow to anger, being too good-natured and dreamy ever to feel the need for self-immolation, which is the root of all choler. But after his childhood admiration for his parents there had been two deeply-felt affections in his life: his love for his daughter, and his friendship for Philip. The golden boy, with the quick lashing wit and the great garden to play in, had not changed in Mr Quill's eyes with the years. Philip would always be rich, happy, elegant and remote; Mr Quill would always feel clumsy beside him, and happy in his awkwardness. They complemented each other. No dark passage had ever marred their relationship; no fumbling in the shrubbery of the O'Connor's garden; no experiments with sex; no dirty conversations with glazed eyes, trembling knees and searching hands. Nothing that was not good, and full of laughter, and a certain brotherly tenderness. Or so it seemed to Mr Quill. It was a friendship that had not faltered on his side for thirty years; and there was no reason why it should not last until the end of their lives.

And now the two people he loved most had betrayed him. About Caroline he could not as yet bring himself to think; but Philip he would gladly at that moment have killed—in his imagination, for he was not a passionate man. He clenched and unclenched his great fists, which had never been used to hurt anybody, and stared down at the carpet. He felt a curious physical excitement which was new to him, and which he could not explain. It was the excitement that is always roused by ill-fortune and pain in those whose nature is essentially passive. For Mr Quill, although he knew as little about his own nature as he did about the character and motives of others, was an introvert. His lies, his dreams of romantic exploits, his boasting and his refusal to face facts, were the defences he used against a world in which he had always felt a little afraid. He did not know that it was Philip who had directed his uncertain and questioning nature into its final mould: Philip who had always been so much more decisive and selfish. If Mr Quill had been as firm of character as he was of body he would not long ago have allowed himself to be dominated by an ideal conceived in a summer garden; an ideal that had grown with the years, like a seed planted at birth in our honour, in the shadow of whose spreading branches we come for shade at the end of our lives. And he would not now sit in despair with murder in his heart at the collapse of that ideal. We all make our own tragedies;

and we are never reconciled to the fact that we have nurtured them in our hearts.

Sybil and her husband felt that they had been cruelly wronged; and for no cause. They did not see what had really happened to them. They could not as yet imagine the empty house when Caroline was gone. They did not see themselves growing old alone; living together only out of habit, with their dreams—harmless and snobbish in Sybil's case, romantic in Mr Quill's—shattered and broken about them. They did not see that as the years passed the tragedy that now loomed before them would become almost a welcome ghost: the only grudge they could share against a world that had passed them by. They would never realize that what had happened meant nothing whatever to anybody except themselves.

But at that moment, and perhaps for the first time in their lives, they were together and at one. Sybil stirred in her chair and looked at her husband, and felt the desire to take him in her arms. Instead she suggested a cup of tea.

'Oh, no, no, no,' said Mr Quill, remembering his stomach, and all the whiskey he had drunk, 'I couldn't face tea.'

'Well, I'll make some for myself.' But she made no move to go to the kitchen.

'I could do with a drop of brandy.'

'There isn't any in it, John.'

They fell silent. Both felt disinclined to go to bed, for they knew that they would not sleep. It was a long time since Mr Quill had spent an entire evening with his wife. They did not quite know what to talk about; and they were both too tired and sick to discuss Caroline and Philip again.

'Is there a pack of cards in it?' asked Mr Quill suddenly.

'Is there what?' Sybil was startled.

'A pack of cards. There used to be one in the sideboard in the dining-room.' In the early years of their marriage the Quills used to entertain in the first flush of the legacy, and the evening often ended with a game of whist or poker. 'I thought we might play a game of poker. I'm not going to sleep tonight. I think I must have got bad whiskey at Paul's birthday party.'

'I'll go and see,' said Sybil briskly. Any idea for passing the time that night would have seemed excellent to her. After a while she came back with a grubby pack and handed them to her husband. 'I don't know if they're all in it,' she said doubtfully.

'It doesn't matter,' said Mr Quill, shuffling them.

'I thought you could only play poker with four people,' said Sybil, pulling out a small table from beside the wall, and placing it between them.

'Not at all. You can play it with two. I'll show you.'

Sybil sat down and watched her husband deal her a hand. But before she picked it up she rose again, and going over to the window drew back the curtains. Nothing could be more reassuring than the sight of a husband and wife playing cards at night in their own home. Outside the road was deserted; and the occupants of the few cars that passed were borne past too quickly to see Mr Quill and his wife playing simplified poker in the small hours of the morning. And of course Sybil would never believe that the people who lived in the houses opposite had never heard of her.

23

MISS LEE was wondering how she might bring Mr Quill to bed. In her experience there were only three kinds of men. Firstly, the ones for whom she was not the right type. They were always the most attractive; but it was just one of those things a girl had to face in life. Then there were the homosexuals. They were also sometimes attractive; and once or twice Miss Lee had made a fool of herself over them. But once she found out she did not worry any more; her honour was saved: no other woman would get them either. And lastly there were the men who played hard to get. (There was actually a fourth type: those who were violently attracted to Miss Lee. But for some reason which she had never bothered to analyse, she discounted these completely. They bored her.)

She decided that Mr Quill was one of the men who played hard to get. He was clearly not a homosexual; and if he was not her type, why did he go on seeing her? And why was he always so polite? And why had he knocked down another man when he insulted her? And why had he taken the loan from her? In Miss Lee's experience the men who took money from a girl without being interested in her were never seen a second time. But Mr Quill not only was there the very next night; he kept on insisting that he would pay back the money.

On the other hand he had never made any kind of a pass at her. Miss Lee knew them all; and she was quite sure that she had not missed one. It was all very puzzling. She was very much excited. She was also at sea. For the plain truth was that she did not know her Irishmen. Like a great many of her compatriots she had dropped her nationality overboard somewhere in the middle of the Irish Sea.

Miss Lee had gone to England when she was sixteen. She stayed with relations for a while in Liverpool, got a job in a factory, and then moved to London. After that she never looked back. She found her true centre in the beauty business. Sweeping up hairs, washing basins, carrying tea-trays, and standing guard over bored Pekinese—those were the days before the rise of the poodle—in a fashionable salon in Conduit Street. Miss Lee was a shrewd girl and she kept away from the Irish. While they were all right for doing the kind of job that she intended to get out of as soon as she could, she observed that in the beauty world very few of them managed to get to the top. Besides,

Madame Estelle who owned the Salon was a Canadian, and hated the Irish: it gave her particular pleasure to employ them for the dirty work. Iris dedicated herself to her chosen profession. She was eager to learn; and she stayed inside her little scented jungle with the same ruthless purpose as a young actress will confine herself to theatrical pubs, clubs and parties. It was no trouble at all at her age to pick up the pinched, constipated patois with its overtones of South Kensington and its undertones of the Mile End Road that was the *lingua franca* of the hair and skin business. She flattered the senior girls; and was deferential and distant to Monsieur Henri, who was Madame's lover. Besides she had no reason to queer her pitch with him. For Miss Lee had discovered that she liked men; and that men liked her. Ageing hairdressers, with monstrous wives in Finchley, found themselves anxious to pass on a few tricks of the trade to the sweet and suppliant young girl; elderly businessmen whose wives patronized Madame Estelle's establishment were touched by her kindness and her obvious respect for experience; such photographers as were interested in women, and who were cutting their way through the same jungle as Miss Lee, found her a good subject and a good pal. It was all grist to the mill. Men were part of the game, if they could be persuaded to yield a secret here, a fur coat there, and introductions anywhere, provided it was within the profession. Iris learned fast and forgot nothing. In a few years she was able to leave Madame Estelle, and get a bigger job in a more fashionable salon in Knightsbridge. Poodles were coming in and Mayfair was going out. Then she really got down to learning her trade. She had the right hands, the right sort of mind, the right contacts, the right accent. Very soon she was helping to manage the salon; and later, with the help of the chargehand, who had wasted the best years of her life on Monsieur Emile, who liked them young and of the same sex as himself, was able to start up on her own in Hampstead. French names were going out, England was coming into its own in the arts: they called the salon Churchill's. They prospered. Her partner took to the bottle and sold out her interest for a fraction of its worth. At twenty-nine Miss Lee had achieved what she wanted. She worked hard; time passed quickly and profitably; in three years she had another salon in Guildford, and then yet another in Brighton. Brighton was now 'in'. Miss Lee at thirty-four was prosperous, busy and shining of visage. But for some curious reason she was not happy. For she had never found the right sort of man. Not that she was ever without one, when it did not interfere with business: men who made love to her because she was pretty, or because they had got into the habit of love-making; men who cultivated her because she was influential in the profession; men who went to Brighton with her and waited in the lounge of the Albion while she inspected her salon, because she paid for them. Lots of men, all English, all knowing exactly what they wanted. But it was never the same thing as Iris wanted; for the simple reason that outside the beauty business she had never had time to discover what it was she wanted.

And then she won five hundred pounds on the Pools, four days before her thirty-fifth birthday. She began to think that she deserved a long holiday; and like many of her compatriots when they achieve success, she began to think of Ireland. She had never given it much thought before. But now she was secure; her business was on a good system; the dread shadow of forty sometimes beckoned her across her shoulder in the many mirrors of her establishments: she would go home. Besides, Ireland had made a small name for itself in the couture business; Miss Lee now sometimes dropped a hint to her more broad-minded customers that she had Irish connections, and found it well received. After nearly twenty years Ireland seemed to her bathed in a golden glow of innocence and youth. The submerged spirit of her race, so long suppressed, suddenly blossomed, and gave forth a wide and heavy perfume.

Englishmen, when all was said and done, were rather dull. They had nothing to say for themselves; not like the lilting-voiced men with their husky laughter, and their mad fits of melancholy and boisterousness, that she remembered in her youth; and sometimes saw represented on the English stage, full of recklessness and sexual daring. So she packed her bags and went home for an indefinite holiday; not without an unexpressed but exciting conviction that something wonderful would happen to her.

And at the end of two months she found herself waiting alone in Mick's for Mr Quill to come in.

He had not been in for three nights and Miss Lee was worried. Neither had Paul. If she had not been so taken up with her own affairs she would have noticed that the friendship between her uncle and Mr Quill had weakened. Mr Quill was dreamy and preoccupied, a condition that she attributed to her own influence; Paul was silent, and mostly incapable of speech. But Miss Lee was in love. She occupied a lighted stage alone with her Johnny. The wings were dark, and beyond the glaring footlights the rest of the world was a mass of blank anonymous faces.

But now all thoughts of her uncle, of her own loneliness, and of the business she would have to return to soon were swept away in a rush of girlish excitement. For Mr Quill had just come in.

'Why, hullo, stranger,' she said brightly, recrossing her legs and smoothing her well-cut heather-tweed suit—Irish couture—over her hips.

Mr Quill raised a finger for the usual and sat down on Paul's chair. He was as neat as ever, but his ruddy face was pale and his eyelids drooped with weariness. Miss Lee thought he had never looked more interesting. She longed to reach out and ruffle his thick black curls, and fasten the button which she noticed was undone in his shining white shirt.

'Well, dear, and where have you been all these years?'

'I've had a bit of a cold,' said Mr Quill, coughing into his fist.

'Oh, you poor boy, you should have a coat. The summer is over.' She looked out at the patch of sky visible above the curtain that discreetly covered the lower half of Mick's front window. The sun was still shining; but for the past week a biting east wind had been sweeping in from the sea. 'Look at me. I had to buy myself an autumn suit. Do you like it? A Maggie MacNamee model. Got herself in Vogue last month, she did.'

Mr Quill looked at her with what seemed to Miss Lee a keener interest than ever before. His heavy eyes flickered over her smart new costume—an adaptation of last season's Balenciaga—and came to rest on the expensive chamois gloves that she had placed on top of her crocodile handbag.

'You look right well,' he said, raising his glass and toasting her. Miss Lee preened herself and smiled happily, vowing that she would pay another visit to Miss Mac-Namee before she went back. And after that there would be frequent weekends in Dublin. A new salon there, perhaps. The old dump really did seem to be cleaning itself up. Her thoughts ran happily on.

'Has Paul been in yet?' Mr Quill went on, looking at the door.

'Why no, dear, Paul hasn't been in either for the last few days. I thought you two boys had gone off on a bat.'

Mr Quill finished his drink and stirred uneasily in his chair.

'Listen,' he said, leaning forward and resting his fore-arms on the table. 'I think we ought to go up to the Green Bar. I'm getting sick of this place. Would you like to come?'

Miss Lee's eyes opened wide, and she tapped her teeth coyly with the rim of her glass. So he doesn't want to meet Uncle Paul, she thought happily. This is going to be a good night. And since Iris was a girl who always lived more in the future than in the present, she began to wonder how much it would cost her to get Mr Quill past the night porter of her hotel. That ancient gentleman did not seem to mind lots of men going up together—Miss Lee had a sharp eye for such things—but she had a notion that he might be difficult with a girl. She cursed herself for staying at such an old-fashioned respectable hotel.

'Wait until I've finished my drink, dear,' she said languidly. 'A girl doesn't like to be hurried.'

Mr Quill kept glancing uneasily at the door, while Miss Lee finished her drink slowly, savouring every moment of the delicious pause. At last she put down her glass, and took up her gloves and bag.

'Let's go,' she said briskly.

In the Green Bar it was noisier than ever. The juke-box was blaring away, surrounded by the usual group of young men, snapping their fingers and swaying their hips to the greasy rhythm. All the tables were occupied and the new comers had to stand in the crowd at the back of the bar.

'Very gay here,' said Miss Lee, laying her hand on Mr Quill's arm to steady herself against the arms, thighs, and shoulders that pressed against her from all sides.

Mr Quill grunted, and drew himself up to his full height to try and catch the barman's eye. When at last he did so and shouted his order over the heads of the people in front of him, he found that his companion had crushed herself against his side, her left breast pressing tightly against his stomach. He stirred uneasily, but he could not move. Miss Lee was smiling up at him, her huge eyes half-closed, her lips parted invitingly. He blinked and looked away towards the bar.

'Oh,' said Miss Lee with a little sigh of pleasure, 'it's hot, dear. But I love it here. So much gayer than that other dump.'

'I hope we get those drinks,' said Mr Quill, wishing very much that he was back in his old place with Paul. He was assailed on all sides by smells: whiskey-laden breaths, sweat, heated tweeds, urine from the lavatory nearby. But most of all he was conscious of Miss Lee. She was wearing a great deal of very expensive scent, which she bought for her salon at wholesale price. It had a lilac foundation, and the effect on Mr Quill was as intoxicating as a large neat Irish. Not only did it trouble his senses; but it stirred up some old obscure memory, long-buried and completely forgotten by his conscious mind. It was the same scent used by the red-haired girl so many years ago when he had followed her out of the train on his first day in Dublin, and found himself in the telephone booth alone over-powered by the synthetic odour that filled the little glass box. Now after twenty-five years he was in the presence of the real thing. And he did not want it.

Confusion often gives courage. As he felt the plum breast pressing closer against his ribs, and the smooth legs caress his calf, he took the plunge.

'Listen,' he said desperately, 'I haven't got that ten pounds to pay you back.'

Miss Lee closed her eyes in simulated boredom.

'Oh, God, not that again. Can't you forget it dear, just for one evening? The way you go on.'

'Well, I'm worried about it. You see—'

'Listen, dear, I'm not exactly a millionairess, but I'm not broke. And I know an honest man when I see you. I'm not worried about that ten pounds. If they don't come with the drinks soon I think we ought to go to my hotel. I've got a bottle of Scotch in my room.'

The invitation was unmistakable; and Mr Quill grew desperate. He made his last throw with the recklessness of the gambler who knows that he has already lost. He knew now that there was plenty of money to be got out of Miss Lee; but he also knew that it would come in small instal-ments. And he had not got the time.

'I've ordered the drinks. We'll have to wait a few min-utes longer.'

'Oh, all right.' She pursed her mouth impatiently and pressed her hand against his chest to steady herself.

'Listen——' he began.

'Yes, dear?'

'I haven't got any money. I don't know if I'll ever be able to pay back that ten pounds.'

'Forget it, dear,' said Miss Lee lightly. But she took her hand away from his chest, and withdrew the tiny shoe which she was carefully insinuating between Mr Quill's feet. It seemed to her suddenly that the music from the juke-box had grown louder; and that she could now hear quite clearly the conversation of her immediate neighbours which a few minutes ago had been inaudible. Our bodies always prepare us for the shock of betrayal; but our imagination, which commands illusion, is rarely as accurate.

'I'll never forget your kindness,' he stumbled on, groping for the words that would make it possible for him to cut himself off forever from his boyhood friend, and from the boy and man he had been himself. But the past can never be wiped out; and our failure to achieve the things we imagine will change our lives and future is in reality the inexorable weight of the pattern life has imposed upon us. If Mr Quill had been in a position to get the money to repay his debt to Philip he would have been a different sort of man; and everything that had happened to him would have happened differently. And so he stood in an agony of embarrassment, tortured by shame, and overcome by the stench of humanity, trapped by himself. 'Listen, could you lend me sixty or seventy pounds? I swear to you I'll pay you back. I'll——'

He could go no further, for the look on Miss Lee's face, which was close enough for him to see it quite clearly, told him what he already knew in his heart. Philip had escaped, as he always had and always would.

The china-doll expression of seductive innocence on Miss Lee's face vanished; and something lean and ruthless took its place. Her eyes narrowed, and her little pouting mouth set in a thin hard line. She seemed suddenly aged; shrewd and impregnable and calculating. What Mr Quill would never know was the cold panic that gripped her mind, or the shame that filled her heart. At that moment they were closer to each other than they had ever been, or ever would be now, in their exact and mutual emotion. But nothing divides two people as inexorably as an identical dilemma that can never be spoken.

Fortunately at that moment the drinks arrived, handed over the heads of the crowd between them and the bar. Mr Quill gave his payment to the man in front for transference along the same route. When he received his change and turned back Miss Lee had gone. He gulped down his drink and made his way with some difficulty to the door.

But Iris Lee had not left the bar. She was standing in front of the juke-box, swaying her hips and snapping her fingers in company with the gay, cautious-eyed young men, with their full mouths and their slanting eyes, who had formed a ring about her. She was performing a version of the Twist for their benefit; a version which she contrived to make at once outrageous and comic. The young men moved closer, smiling at one another; for they understood ladies like Miss Lee perfectly. In her disillusionment she had suddenly discovered a talent which had long been latent within her: she was a natural clown. As she mugged, crossed her eyes, and beat her knees together, the young men moved closer about her, clapping their hands very gently at first. The crowd at the bar turned good-humouredly to watch her. They did not have a free show like this every evening. The circle of young men began to clap their hands louder, and moved closer. Nearer and nearer they came, their narrow eyes shining, until Miss Lee dizzy and sick, collapsed against the juke-box. They helped her to a chair, their soft creamy voices full of solicitude, their arms linked together. Miss Lee would never lack company again.

24

'You shouldn't have written to me like that.'

'It was the only way I had to get in touch with you. I rang the office and they told me you had left. I didn't like to ring your house.'

'I'm going to England.'

'When?'

'Next week.'

'Why didn't you tell me?'

Caroline was silent. She had not wanted to see Philip again; but when his letter arrived telling her that if she did not meet him he would call at her house she took fright and hurried to their old meeting-place, while her mother was at the church.

They were in the drawing-room. It too had changed. The gardener had been in during the morning and removed the dust-covers from the furniture. Windows had been opened; and the old dusty, battened-down smell was almost gone. The Ashtons were coming back.

'Why didn't you tell me?' he insisted.

'What would be the use?' said Caroline wearily, drawing her fingertips across her eyes.

'You're pregnant, aren't you?'

She turned and faced him. She had already acquired something of the dangerous calm of the pregnant woman; something too of the uneasy boldness of those who have transgressed their own rules.

'Yes.'

She did not take her eyes from his face, half-hoping that she would see him humbled. But Philip was only disconcerted by the emotions, and by the trivial irritations of life. The larger issues which had to be faced and surmounted seemed to calm and settle his restless temperament. He took her hand and led her to one of the sofas, and then drew up a chair and sat down in front of her.

'How long?' he asked briskly, with something of the objectivity of a doctor.

'Two months. I think. I'm not quite sure.' She sat bolt upright on the cushions, gripping the edges of them on either side of her.

'I suspected it the last time you were here. Well, it's not too late for something to be done. It's better that you should go to England. It's always dangerous in this country, no matter how much you pay. But it can be arranged safely in London. I'll pay, of course. Then you can come back.'

'I'm not coming back, Philip.'

'It would be better, I think, if you did, especially for your parents' sake. You always told me that you never wanted to go to England, that you wanted to stay in this country. I know you mean that. You'll be all right in a month, and then you can come back. If you don't want to go into your old office I'll arrange something for you in the city.'

So confident and unemotional was his manner that for a moment Caroline felt herself swept away by his matter-of-factness. She had never really seen this side of him: that practical self-assurance that governed every aspect of his life except the emotional. She had sensed it in him at the beginning when he had seemed to offer so much certainty —a certainty that had been denied her all her life by the two people she had had to love—her parents. But Philip could only have provided that certainty if he had taken her ruthlessly, as he had taken all the other women in his life except his wife. No two people ever make love alone. All about them, like shadows in the corner of a room, stand the ghostly presences of those others who have made them what they are. Because for a brief moment and quite unconsciously Philip had sensed in this young girl the reflection of another; had allowed himself the fatal pleasure of retracing an emotion now faded but still irremovable, he had exposed that one corner of his heart that was vulnerable, and wrecked the image that Caroline had created out of her need for love and certainty.

'No, Philip, I'm not coming back.'

'Do your parents know this?'

'Yes.'

'Do they know— ?'

'Yes.'

Philip was silent. He turned away from her and looked through the window on to the garden. Caroline looked at his profile, neat, regular, remote: the image that she would always remember. An oblique image: Philip's head turned away from her, outlined in silhouette against a window etched against the sky above the glittering bay.

He turned back and looked at Caroline with affection. Just as the room in which they sat had suddenly emerged normal and comfortable again from under its ghostly covers, so too Caroline in her ordinary, sordid plight no longer troubled his senses with the mystery of something unexplained and unattainable. He felt for her now, when it was too late, all that paternal anxiety, that firm and confident solicitude that he had been unable to give her when he was her lover. He smiled, and leaning forward took her hand in his.

Caroline too felt her fears melting away; and responded to the pressure of his hand, sensing the firmness of purpose that lay behind it. Love is renounced in a multitude of ways; but never more irrevocably than by accepting our lovers as the sort of people they are, instead of the creatures of fantasy that we create out of our longings and our desires.

'Don't worry,' he said, pressing her hand again before relinquishing it for the last time, 'don't worry at all. Leave it to me. Have you any money?'

'Twenty-seven pounds.'

'Are you going away on that! It's a good thing I insisted on seeing you. This thing will cost at least a hundred, and you'll have to have something left over for a holiday afterwards.' He smiled and shook his head. 'Twenty-seven pounds, my dear girl.'

Caroline was hurt that her money, which she had earned herself and so carefully saved, should have made so little impression on him.

'It's quite sufficient,' she said sharply. 'I'm only buying a single ticket, and when I get to England I'll get a job at once, and I expect to be able to save something out of my wages.'

'But Caroline it would take you ages to get the money together, and by then it would be too late. You must have this operation at once.'

Caroline, who had been staring down at the carpet, looked up in genuine amazement.

'What operation?'

Philip was taken aback. He blinked before her steady gaze, and fingered his tie nervously.

'But surely you don't want to have this baby, do you? I mean to say, you couldn't possibly. It would be dreadful.'

'Yes I do mean to have this baby, Philip,' she said quietly.

'But—'

'Is that what you've been offering me money for? An abortion? Is that it?'

'But surely you can't go through with this? What would you do with the child? Your whole life—'

'I'm not going to have an abortion, Philip,' said Caroline steadily, instinctively placing her folded hands under her breast, and starting back from him. 'I'm going to get a job in England, and work as long as I can, and then I'm going to go through with it. I'm not going to commit murder.'

Philip stared at her in amazement for a few moments, and then got up and walked to the window.

'Caroline, do you really mean this?' he said at length in a low, halting voice.

'Yes, Philip, I mean it.' The life which she was carrying within her, and which had caused her so much terror and

165

anguish, seemed to stir and fill her with courage. She no longer felt ashamed, or even very frightened. She had not planned how she would face this thing alone, because she could not bring herself to think about it. Now suddenly she was filled with a kind of exaltation: that sense of wonder at the mysterious ripeness of her own body, which financial necessity and social pressure can sometimes numb, but never entirely destroy in any woman. She was fighting for a life; compared with which her love for Philip seemed curiously far away and unimportant.

Guilt is a male emotion; and Philip was seized with a devouring remorse. It was all he could do to prevent himself hurrying to her side in utter abjection. But he was saved by his sense of the practical and business-like nature of their new relationship. He had inherited a sense of responsibility; and it did not occur to him to try to take the easy way out of this affair, for which he blamed himself entirely. Caroline would have to be cared for, protected, and given a chance to start life again. If she insisted on this crazy idea of having an unwanted baby, she must be helped in every possible way.

But he made a last effort to dissuade her.

'Do you know what this means, Caroline? Do you realize what you are letting yourself in for? What are you going to do when it's all over?'

'I don't know, I haven't thought about it. What's the use of making plans? I'll manage, don't worry. One always does.'

'But Caroline, I can't let you do this! You can't go away like this from your home just because of me,' he said, coming back from the window and standing in front of her.

She looked up at him. Her face was pale and expressionless.

'It's not because of you Philip, it's because of myself.'

'Oh, God,' he groaned, covering his forehead with his hand. 'Well, at least let me pay. There'll be expenses—'

'In England you get medical attention free.'

'But this child is mine as well as yours. I'm responsible for it.'

'I don't think you are, Philip. You see, you never loved me. I thought for a little while that you did, and it's because of that that I'm going to have this baby.'

He looked at her with something like wonder. Could this calm woman be the awkward girl that he had first brought to this house a few short months ago?

'So I took you because you were young and inexperienced, is that what you think?' he said bitterly.

'No, I don't think that. If I did I'd take your money and do what you ask. But I loved you—' her voice broke, and she paused for a few moments to pull herself together. Philip looked at her closely. He was a man who in the last resort relished his power over others; and he did not care to be humbled. If she broke down now he knew that she would escape only on his terms. But Caroline seemed to read what was in his mind, and she shook her head with a little smile, and went on:

'I suppose in a way I'll always love you. But it wasn't me you loved, Philip. It's strange, but I think it was this house that first made me realize it. I remember reading somewhere that houses have souls. I thought it silly at the time, but now I'm sure. You were trying to recapture something, weren't you? Something that happened here long ago.'

We are so unsure of our own motives that when we are told the truth about ourselves it sometimes seems far more incredible than anything we can invent about others.

'That isn't true,' Philip burst out passionately.

'Isn't it?'

Caroline got up and walked across the room. As he watched her go it seemed to Philip that he had never known her more formidable and remote. But the hands which the girl kept pressed against her thighs were trembling, and she knew that she was very near to hysteria. She knew that if she did not leave she would relinquish the only hope she had of facing the future: the hope that grows out of desperation and pride. And the only way she had of preserving something intact out of the wreck of her love for Philip was to reject any offer of help from him.

But Philip, intimidated by her unexpected inflexibility, her sudden assumption of mature dignity, stood silent and helpless before her. His sensitivity to the moods of others was aroused only by sexual desire. He could not sense behind the proud and pathetic face the final weakness that assailed her. He was trapped, as Mr Quill had been as he struggled for something to say to Miss Lee, by the sort of man he was. All he could think of offering Caroline now was money; the tribute for which her father had pleaded and shamed himself. If he had reverted to that self-confident mood with which he had gained Caroline's trust a short while before, he might have renewed his hold over her. At the moment of parting all the illusions we have cherished rise up and strangle our will, like the crisis in a long-drawn-out illness. A glance, a touch, a tear is enough to destroy all our resolutions.

But Philip was incapable of that sensual and instinctive penetration which would have drawn Caroline back to him. She had intimidated him by her sudden revelation of a truth he could not accept. For Philip, in his own fashion, imagined that he had loved her. And so the moment passed and dissolved; and the present hardened between them.

'Will you write to me at least?' he said in an uncertain, embarrassed tone. 'Will you let me know how you are getting on? I can't let you go away with so little money. Let me give you—'

'I have enough money, Philip,' said Caroline with that touch of cruelty which no woman can resist when she sees her lover revealed as the ordinary mortal he is. 'But I'll write to you and tell you how I am when it's all over.'

Philip, unable to bear the thought of anybody facing such a future with so little money—the rich distrust the whole world only a little less than paupers—turned away and walked to the window to conceal his impotent concern. He did not hear her leave the room; and he made no move to follow her as he watched her pass the window and disappear round the turn of the avenue.

He stood for a long time staring out at the garden, green-grey under the lowering sky, and empty now even of shadows; hearing nothing but the tiny creaking of the old house about him, and the whispering of the laburnum outside. Then he turned back into the room, pale-faced and alone. Mr. Quill was avenged. But he would never know it.

25

LILIAN, smelling the brandy, had sent the two boys into the garden the moment she came into the room. Miss Blake was clearly a little drunk, a condition which sharpened rather than dulled her brain, and transformed her malice into viciousness. Lilian stood at the open window looking after them. Tom had stopped and was bending over a rose-bush with his hands clasped behind his back, half-lost in the trance of concentration into which he sometimes fell. Phil was walking down the path with a curious stealthy stiff-legged walk. He was stalking a pigeon he had spotted in the strawberry beds.

'Nice to have the boys back,' said Miss Blake sweetly, her voice only a little thickened by brandy. She was in fact very far from being drunk; but she had observed Lilian's disapproval and resolved to live up to it. She was sitting in her chair smoking, one hand over the arm-rest to reassure herself that the bottle and glass, which she had hastily concealed at the side, were still intact. 'Did they enjoy themselves in Winchester?'

'Yes, very much.' Lilian turned back and sat down opposite the old woman.

'So you brought them along to pay their respects. Very civil of you, dear. Except of course that I didn't get an opportunity to bid them the time of day. I hope they don't injure my roses.'

'They won't. I thought it better not to let them see you drunk. They can come another time.' Lilian lit a cigarette.

'I'm nothing of the sort,' said Rose hotly. She didn't mind in the least shocking Lilian by the smell of brandy, but she detested having her less reputable activities put into words by other people. When Rose was a little tight she intended that the world should be told it by herself. 'How dare you!'

'The room reeks of brandy.'

'Oh, is that what you mean, dear? Well, why didn't you say so in the first place? I hate furtive people. That weedy little curate called before you came and I gave him a glass of brandy to tone up his virility. I was thinking of his wife —so over-sexed and nothing to show for it.'

Lilian made no reply. Miss Blake took out a very dirty checked handkerchief and held it to her nose as if she had got a bad smell.

'I suppose you know that girl is expecting a baby,' she said, her voice muffled by the handkerchief. 'The Quill girl, dear, not the curate's wife.'

'Yes. That's one of the reasons I called. I was prepared for it.'

'Who told you?' demanded the old woman pettishly, taking the handkerchief from her nose and stuffing it down in the chair beside her. 'I knew it a week ago. I could see there was something wrong with the mother, so I got it out of her—'

'And you told Dolly Abberton, who told a friend who told me. The usual Dublin grapevine. You're losing your touch, Rose. A few years ago you'd have saved it up as a special treat for me.'

'That Dolly Abberton, the old cow. She swore on her oath—'

'And her oath is of the same ilk as yours, Rose.'

Rose looked at her with narrowed eyes, and then chuckled fatly.

'Well, this is a nice kettle of fish, I must say. I never expected that, not in my wildest dreams. Whatever can Philip have been thinking of? And you say I'm losing my touch. By the way, how is he?'

'Quite well. I'm afraid I have no scenes, or hysterics to report.'

'Are they going to follow him for money? It'll cost him a pretty penny to keep that out of the courts.'

'I don't know what they're going to do. I suppose Philip will pay. It's the least he might do.'

'I expect it was he arranged this trip to England. It's the routine procedure, isn't it? She can get rid of it, and then come back if she wants to.'

Lilian, who had anticipated every remark that Rose might make, including what she had just said, was nevertheless unable to conceal her discomfiture. She made no reply; and Rose knew she had scored.

'We'll just have to wait and see, dear,' she went on happily. 'If they fix it up between them, it probably means she'll be back.'

'I'm sure you won't have to wait long, Rose,' said Lilian acidly. 'I'm sure you'll worm that out of the mother too.'

'Of course, dear. Especially since you want me to.'

Lilian stood up abruptly and walked back to the window. Tom was standing in the middle of the path looking up at the house, his pale, oval-shaped face tilted back. Lilian thought again with a little pang how very like her father he was. Phil had disappeared into the shrubbery.

Behind her Rose began to chuckle to herself, a wheezing,

sinister little sound, rather like the choking of a sick child.

'Of course the whole thing is comic, dear, isn't it?' she said at length when Lilian made no move to turn round or to speak.

'Comic?' Lilian spun round and stared angrily at the old woman. 'Comic!'

'Well it is. Getting a girl with child in this day and age. It used to be a terrible tragedy when I was a girl, and I daresay it still is down the country where the Quills come from, and where everybody knows everybody else. But I can't take it seriously, really I can't. It's too funny.'

Lilian came back and sat down again. She was angry; but she was no longer unsure of herself. She put her cigarettes on the chair between them, and savoured the greedy look which Rose gave them.

'So you think it's funny, Rose,' she said, tapping ash into the saucer ashtray. 'There's nothing comic about it I can assure you. Of course I'm not a Catholic and I wouldn't blame the girl for getting rid of it. It's no fun facing life with a bastard no matter how much you get paid for it, and it's even less fun signing one away to foster-parents. All the same I hope she has the courage to have it, even if people do laugh. I've noticed that people usually laugh at something they're afraid of, and a great many people are afraid of life nowadays. So I suppose they have to make it comic.'

'Noble sentiments, dear. They do you credit to be sure. But are they trotted out to put an old spinster in her place?'

'Partly,' said Lilian, pushing the packet of cigarettes towards Rose. 'Here, have one of these. They'll help to smother the smell of brandy.'

'Sweet of you, dear. The curate gave me one of his cigarettes too. People are too kind. But then you're in a very sweet and kind mood today. I shouldn't be at all surprised if you went down to the boat to see the girl off. After all Philip can hardly do it, can he?' She thumped her chest and began to search in the depths of the chair for her handkerchief.

'I admit I'm glad she's going, if that's what you want me to say. And I hope she stays there too. But I'm sorry for her, and I hope Philip treats her well. It's horrible for her, and for her parents too.'

'Sweeter and sweeter, dear. I'm lapping it up. I feel a little soiled and cynical in the presence of such saintly forbearance, I really do. However, if your prayers are answered, and she has the baby, I doubt if she'll come back. They never do when they go through with it to the bitter end. But if she gets rid of it, you can expect her back on an early boat, to take up where she left off. Yes, indeed, dear. I've often noticed that noble sentiments are apt to have a vested interest somewhere. It's a wonder that you haven't gone over to Rome years ago with Philip.' Rose exhaled smoke contentedly, and followed its slow ascent towards the ceiling with narrowed eyes. She was beginning to enjoy herself. She burrowed back into her chair and spread her fat thighs like a man.

'I'll say one thing for you, Rose, you have a genius for giving things an original twist.'

Rose lowered her massive head and waved her hand in front of her face to clear the smoke. Then she looked at Lilian with attention. There was no sparkle of malice in her eyes, no cynical smile on her lips: she seemed to Lilian suddenly very formidable. There were times when the old woman had a sort of remote dignity, as if she were remembering a lesson learned long ago when she had been brought up to assume that she and her circle of friends were set apart by the dispensation of providence to rule a commoner clay.

'Perhaps,' she said slowly, 'perhaps. I've been told that so often. And yet I wonder. It's always said to me by people who are hanging on to something because they're afraid. Sooner or later most of them make a speech about life being one big muddle anyhow, and let's make the most

173

of it. And if they have a husband they don't give a damn about any more, or who doesn't give a damn about them, they'll tell you that it's better than living in a bed-sitter on your own. And if they have children they'll let you know that it's better than not having them. You know the sort of thing, dear? You should, because that's exactly what you're thinking now. I've heard it all before, and it bores me because it isn't true.'

'Isn't it?'

Rose lifted her shoulders and covered her mouth with her hand to smother a belch.

'I've no doubt that you do feel sorry for the silly child. But you're like all the rest of them, you won't face the truth. You don't really give a rap about Philip any more, except that he's your property. All this love business, it makes me sick. When you're young it's an excuse to climb into bed, and when you're old it's something to take like a drug to keep you from facing the fact that nobody gives a damn about you. It's like believing in God because you're afraid of hell.'

'I don't think it's as simple as that, Rose. Maybe there isn't much left now between Philip and me. But there was something once, and it was good while it lasted. And now there are the children.' Lilian looked over her shoulder; but she could not see Tom from where she was sitting.

'Exactly, dear. I've seen that coming for a long time. Now that Philip is gone you're going to fasten on to Tom, because after all he's yours, and the only person we ever really love is ourself. All the rest is sheer hypocrisy.'

'Children have got to be protected,' said Lilian sharply.

'Mother love has got to be protected, dear. It's part of the code. Oh, what's the use! It's a waste of time talking to people like you.' The old woman reverted to her old pettish manner, and thumped the arm of the chair with her fist.

'I'm afraid it is,' said Lilian with a smile. 'After all I don't see what can be done about it. I have an unfaithful husband, and I've got two children. I don't know what I can do for Philip at this time of day. Perhaps I've failed him in some way, perhaps he'd be the same no matter who he married. I don't know. But I don't want Tom to start hating his father because of me. I can't see any farther than that at the moment.'

Rose snorted.

'In other words you're going to go on sacrificing yourself for Philip. That's what it boils down to, dear. And you'll get left in the lurch in the end, like all the rest of us. Tom will leave you too, you know, even if he turns out to be a mother's boy. They're the worst of all. They eat their mothers.'

Lilian laughed. She felt quite light-hearted and almost gay, and realized now why it was that she kept coming back to Rose. Not only because behind all the malice the old woman was fond of her, and she was a link with the happy past; but she had helped her in her own way to go on facing life. Just now Rose had made her admit to herself that she no longer wanted Philip as a lover; and that she was an incurable optimist. A few weeks ago she had shivered in this room and wondered if she would become as bitter and loveless as Rose. But she knew now that she would always snatch at every straw; always keep on hoping that things would turn out all right; always go on wanting somebody to care for.

We never realize our own nature until we meet its exact opposite.

She looked at her old friend with affection; understanding that Rose too, in her own oblique way, wanted her. There would always be somebody who did.

'Well,' she said lightly, 'It's not much of a future, is it? I think the only thing left for me is to take a lover myself. What do you think, Rose.

The old woman chuckled. She knew she had lost a disciple, and kept a friend.

'It would be the price of Philip, dear, it really would. And I can fix you up with one any time you like.'

'I don't think I'm too old to get one for myself, Rose. But who do you suggest?'

'Mr Quill, dear. He's randy enough for anything. Such goings on in all the bars of Dun Laoghaire! And this little tart he's running after at the moment is forty if she's a day. So you'd qualify.'

'I think after that Rose you might give me a glass of brandy. I know you've got it hidden behind the chair.'

Rose glared at her for a moment, and then slowly heaved herself up, and waddled over to the bookcase. She poked about behind the rows of Victorian classics, and ambled back hugging the bottle to her bosom like a baby, and holding two glasses by their stems between her fingers.

'I've got no such thing hidden behind the chair,' she said, putting down the glasses beside the packet of cigarettes, and uncorking the bottle. 'What do you think I am?'

'That's enough, Rose, thank you. I've got to drive home.'

'I keep it in the bookcase because of Anderson,' said Rose, settling into her chair again. 'If the old cow got her hands on it she'd be drunk for a week.' She raised her glass. 'Well, here's to the mail-boat, dear. If we must be happy, let's be happy, even if it's at somebody else's expense. It usually is.'

Rose always kept her most poisonous darts for the end, and she grinned happily as she watched the younger woman's face cloud. Then Lilian lifted her head and smiled.

'To you, Rose.'

Rose nodded and swallowed her brandy noisily, wiping her lips with her fingers. She had no intention of letting Lilian transform her into an old harmless reprobate, whose bark is worse than her bite.

'Thank you, dear, it's nice to hear that, even if you can

afford to be generous at the moment. And we'll have another glass when I fix you up with Mr Quill. He'll be on the loose quite soon, because I intend to tell his wife all. The poor woman, it's a shame to see her being made such a fool of. I think wives ought to be told, don't you?'

Lilian put down her glass and stood up. Rose had brought it off again, as she always would.

'I told you that if you do this I'll never speak to you again,' she said angrily. 'I mean that, Rose.'

'I know, dear,' said Rose, as she uncorked the bottle. 'I'll be seeing you.'

Lilian picked up her cigarettes and walked out onto the terrace. Rose got up unsteadily and went over to the window. Lilian was walking down the steps to greet her sons who were hurrying up the path to meet her. She held out her hands to them, patting Phil on the shoulder and ruffling Tom's hair. Then the trio walked round the end of the house to the car.

Rose Blake sipped her brandy. She was in no way disconcerted by this display of family solidarity. Besides she was thinking of what she was going to say to Mrs Quill. And children bored her.

26

MR QUILL sat in his dining-room holding an evening paper in front of him. But he was not reading it. From the kitchen came the sounds of running water and the clatter of dishes as Caroline washed up after the tea. Sybil had gone to visit Miss Blake. She had spent a great deal of her time during the past week with the old woman; and Mr Quill was already aware of a profound change in his wife's attitude towards him. She had said nothing definite; but from several heavy hints that she had dropped while Caroline was out of the house, he surmised that it had something to do with Miss Lee. The storm, he knew, was gathering; but for the moment, during the few days that remained before Caroline went away, it would not break. When it did it would only confirm the guilt that Mr Quill already felt: and guilt was something he had never suffered from in his life. From now on, he thought, everything was going to be very different.

He put down his paper and stared gloomily out the window. The little lawn was now hopelessly overgrown; and weeds choked the border under the cement wall at the end of the garden. For the first time in his life Mr Quill no longer made a mental reservation that sometime, next day, next week, he would cut the lawn and weed the garden. He now knew that he would never do it.

Caroline came back into the room, wiping her hands in a towel. She looked at her father, put the towel down on the sideboard, and came and sat down beside him at the table. She reached out and took his hand, and pressed it gently. Mr Quill shaded his eyes with his other hand, and stared down at a photograph of a huge man in short white togs and a striped jersey, poised in mid-air in a curiously epicene posture as he leaped to catch a football.

'Don't worry, Daddy,' said Caroline softly, 'I'll be all right.'

'It'll be terrible lonely in the house without you,' said Mr Quill, digging his little finger into the corner of his eye, and hunching his shoulders.

Caroline made no reply, but clutched her father's hand still harder.

'Your mother seems to blame me for all of it,' said Mr Quill, unable to resist talking about the frightening change in Sybil, the real reason for which he could not possibly disclose.

'Of course she doesn't, Daddy. She's just worried, that's

all. It was the same way when the other girls in the office went away. Carmel O'Leary's mother cried for three days, but now she doesn't mind at all because Carmel got such a good job in England, and Mrs O'Leary is going over to spend a holiday with her next month.'

'It's not the same, Carry.' Mr Quill withdrew his hand from his daughter's, and clasped both fists over his eyes. It was the first allusion he had made to his daughter's circumstances. Caroline felt suddenly cold and miserable; but her father's distress gave her courage. She drew a circle on the polished table with her forefinger, and concentrated on it; while Mr Quill used the photograph of the footballer to cover his embarrassment.

'I know it's not the same, Daddy. But it's no good talking about it. I'm sorry.'

Mr Quill made no reply, but he slowly disengaged one hand and reached out blindly towards his daughter. Caroline took it in her two hands and held it fast.

'I could kill him,' he whispered, turning over a page and staring at two other epicene giants apparently embracing each other in mid-air.

'No, Daddy, no.' Caroline lifted her father's hand and shook it.

But Mr Quill was already overwhelmed with self-pity.

'My best friend for thirty years to do this to me. And I thought I knew him. I'd have trusted him with anything. I didn't think a thing like this could happen to anybody.'

Caroline leaned forward, crouching over her father's hand as she might over a sick baby.

'Daddy, don't hate anybody. Don't let yourself get like that. It won't do any good, honest it won't. We've all got a long time to live yet, please God, and all this will pass. Don't think about it too much. Nobody gets away very long without some trouble. Wouldn't it be worse if you or Mammy got sick or had an accident or something? Look at the people in the terrace here. There's not a family but has lost somebody. At least we still have one another.'

179

'No, we haven't. We've lost you. You'll never come back, I know you won't. And your mother thinks I'm to blame for the whole thing. I suppose I am too in a way. He was my friend.'

'Nobody's to blame, Daddy,' said Caroline firmly, 'except me.'

Mr Quill lifted the page of the newspaper and began to tear it into strips slowly with his free hand. The white togged giants were sundered; but not entirely: one of them surrendered his legs and part of his arms to the other.

'Well, your mother blames me, and it's not going to get any better with her as time goes on. She's that kind of woman. When her mother died she blamed her father, and she never forgave him. Now she won't believe anything I say any more. I can't go out of the house for a walk or a drink, but she thinks I'm going someplace else. She watches me like I was a thief or something. And when you're not here any more, I don't know how it's going to be.'

In the sincerest misery that we suffer for another we rarely forget ourselves. Mr Quill loved his daughter deeply. In his little world, about which he had woven such a rich and multi-coloured fantasy, there had always been a hard centre of truth: Caroline, Sybil, Philip. And now, in one swift stroke, he had lost all of them. He was not an insensitive man; and he was more easily intimidated by the unspoken than by the spoken. Like all people who create a world of fantasy for themselves, he trusted others far more than he trusted himself. And he knew now that he was trapped. Sybil, when all the arguing and explaining were over, would never really trust him again. She would be hurt; and Mr Quill could never bear to hurt anybody. In the light of the baleful helplessness that he knew his wife was capable of, all his little pleasures would become furtive. He would never be able to believe his own lies again in the only place where anybody had ever taken them seriously: his own home.

Caroline tightened her grip on her father's hand; but some of the tension in her arched body eased. It is always easier to have courage for two. She lifted his hand and held it against her cheek. It was cold and damp, and as she tried to warm it something of her courage and sympathy communicated itself to Mr Quill more effectively than words could ever have done. He lifted his head from the newspaper and looked at his daughter. Caroline was smiling. He reached out his other hand and stroked her hair, as he used to do when she was a little girl. She moved her head under his caress and closed her eyes.

'Caroline,' he said, forgetting all his own troubles in the unspoken current of love and trust that passed between them, 'are you afraid?'

The girl opened her eyes and looked at her father steadily. She wished that she could prolong this moment indefinitely, finding an answer in her blood for all the questions and doubts that assailed her and her parents; dispensing with words that create such confusion. Just as her mother, by taking her in her arms and striking her, had said all that was necessary, so too her father's helpless reaching out of his hand, his tender stroking of her hair, had brought them closer together than they had ever been before. But words, like death, and loneliness and love, are part of our heritage: we cannot escape from them.

'No, Daddy,' she whispered, shaking her head and slipping her fingers through his, 'no, I'm not. And you mustn't be either.'

'But I am, Carry. I'm afraid for you. How are you going to manage over there on your own? And your mother and I can't afford to go over with you.'

'You mustn't worry about me, Daddy. And anyway I couldn't stay at home for the rest of my life. We all have to strike out on our own sometime or another, and, and—' her voice trembled, but she grasped her father's hand to give her courage, and went on—'we're all on our own when you come to think about it. I used to think we weren't, but we are. I can't explain why it is, but I know it now. It's just something that you have to face and make the best of, and not get bitter about.'

Mr Quill looked at his daughter who was so young, and so much wiser than he. And he thought of his own parents that he had loved so well, and forgotten so quickly. Elements that lived still in his bones and his blood; but that he thought about only in moments of sentiment and anger, when he wanted to make a comparison between the happy past and the ruthless present. He thought of Philip, that he had trusted and loved and thought he knew. He thought of his wife, and wondered how he would cope with her now that they were alone together for the rest of their lives. After twenty years Mr Quill realized that he knew as little about Sybil as he knew about anybody else. And lastly he thought of his daughter. Could this calm, pale-faced woman be the little girl that he loved ? And in his despair and bewilderment he envied her, in spite of the desperate situation she found herself in: a situation he could not even yet call by its name, lest the awful reality of it should overwhelm him. We can never imagine anybody else being as lonely as ourselves.

'Oh, Carry,' he burst out, grasping at the only illusion he had left, 'you're young, and you're going to make a new life for yourself. You're clever and you're beautiful, and some day you'll get married, and you'll forget all about this. I know you will, and I know you'll be happy.'

Caroline, who had so early discovered the necessity for juggling with words, realized now that even at the moment of parting she would have to lie to her father, if she was to leave him with something of the courage she had found in herself.

'Yes, Daddy, I'll forget about it. It'll pass, you'll see.'

'And you'll write, Carry, won't you ? Regular, every week.'

'Of course I will, Daddy. You mustn't worry. Women are not quite as helpless as you think. They adapt themselves, you know, like cats. And they're tough too. All the girls I know that went to England settled down very quickly, far better than the men. And then maybe next year you and Mammy will be able to come over and visit me.'

'Oh, we will, Carry, next year for sure. Maybe even at Christmas.'

Caroline did not reply. She knew that she would spend Christmas alone. Mr Quill suddenly realized the reason for her silence, and glanced down at his torn footballers again.

'Daddy, would you like me to make another cup of tea ?'

Mr Quill shook his head. At this hour in the old days he would already have been in Mick's. Paul would be sitting on his book, giving his acid attention to his friend's romantic dreams of love. How often in the counterpoint that makes up even the slightest relationship had he protested against Paul's view of life. Life, Mr Quill was in the habit of declaring, was beautiful.

'Life is hell,' he said now. 'That's what it is.'

'No, Daddy, that's not true. It's bad and it's good, often at the same time,' said Caroline haltingly. She was responding to her father's mood, rather than expressing any conscious system of her own. At the moment she was incapable of thinking coherently about anything except the need to keep herself from crying out in anguish and despair. She did not know that she had the one thing that makes life bearable, and even meaningful: courage. What she was giving back to her father now was the love that she had always received from him: the love that she would always seek, and the certitude that she would never find. 'But it's not hell, unless you make it that way yourself. Don't start hating everything and everybody just because of me.'

'It isn't because of you, Carry. I didn't mean that.'

'I know you didn't, Daddy. But it is because of me all the same. It's all my fault. It would never have happened if I had thought about you and Mammy, and how well off I was. Now I know how lucky I was. But maybe I'd never have realized it if this hadn't happened. You always loved life, because you liked people. Don't start hating them now, don't please. I couldn't bear that. It's bad enough as it is.'

'Oh, Carry, if I could only do something for you. If I only had real money to give you instead of that lousy five-pound note—'

'I have enough money, more than enough.'

'No, you haven't. It's awful to think of you going to England with only a few pounds in your pocket.'

'I have thirty-two pounds. Twenty-seven of my own and the five you gave me.' Caroline's voice was sharp. 'Why does everybody keep on talking about money?' she burst out.

'Because money makes you independent,' said Mr Quill bitterly. 'If you have it you don't have to ask anybody for anything. You don't have to put yourself in anybody's power. Nobody can hurt you if you have money.'

'Yes, they can,' said Caroline quietly.

'But it won't be always like this,' said her father, warming to his theme. 'From now on I'll be able to save a little, and when I do—' he broke off and clenched his fist over the tattered newspaper.

'You and Mammy will come over and visit me, won't you ?' said Caroline quickly.

'I have a good deal of debts to pay off, Carry. But when I do we'll be over all right. Next summer.'

'Next summer. Promise.'

'I promise.'

Caroline looked out at the overgrown garden, with its broken trellis, erected in a moment of expansion long ago, to which a ragged carpet of roses still clung. And as she looked, remembering another garden, the gates of which were now closed to her forever, she felt the strength that her father's weakness had summoned up in her, weakening. She knew that her parents would not come to visit her next summer; that her pride and her fear would prevent her from coming back for a long time; and that when she did come back everything would be changed. She looked miserably at the roses, hopeful, tenacious roses that often in that wild garden held up a candle for the spring in the November gloom.

Mr Quill felt something of his old confidence return as he persuaded himself that he and Sybil would go to England for their holidays next year. He had never been there: it would be a real break. And then, as he thought about it, with something of the hopeful desperation of a schoolboy thinking of Christmas on the last day of the summer holiday, he became aware of something immediate and frightening. His hand had warmed in Caroline's; hers had grown stiff and icy. She kept her head averted from him, looking out of the window, and her whole body seemed frozen with concentration as she sat staring at the shabby little patch of green. Mr Quill knew now that it was his turn to try and give courage to his daughter.

'Don't worry, Carry,' he said firmly. 'Everything will be all right.'

Caroline did not turn her head. When she spoke it was in the calm, deceptively casual voice that we use when we demand the certainty of truth from a stranger.

'Daddy, you've been through it all. I'm only beginning, and it seems an awful long time to go. People have died belonging to you. You've married and made a home. You always seemed so sure of everything. You must know something about it. Tell me.'

27

IT was the first of September. The sky over Dublin Bay was softened by a golden haze. The sea reflecting the light was yellow, the colour of a tarnished mirror. The air was honey-sweet and its lips were soft. But already the large white butterfly, ghostly harbinger of autumn, was fluttering among the gardens by the sea; and above the sleepy cone of Killiney Hill the swifts were screaming for the end of summer, cleaving the air with their black scimitar wings, heading south. In the squares of the city trees were hunched and laden with gold, like misers at the edge of the grave. But the air was honey-sweet and its lips were soft, and as yet no golden coins were plucked from the branches to scatter upon the echoing pavements.

As the sea reflected the sky, so too along the rim of the bay it darkened, reflecting the dim curving body of the city. The little pirate city of the Norsemen that had stretched itself in the sleep of centuries from the toe of Dalkey to Howth Head. As it slept it dreamed fine dreams. Far away beyond the burnished midland plain the autumn mists were rising from the inland rivers, and coiling about the empty meadows and the houses with the blind windows and the gaping doors. But no damp fingers disturbed the dreaming city, for the air was honey-sweet and its lips were soft. A little shiver rippled through the golden haze of the sky, and the mirror moved, and the city stirred and murmured in its sleep, like a woman repeating the name of her lover. Far away beyond the blue mountains of the west the ravens were croaking on the dead cliffs above the cold Atlantic, already flecked with winter foam. But it was a far sound, and between it the mountains stood guard, and the sleepy plains, and the rich meadows, and the green hills, and the names of saints and soldiers and martyrs, and poets dead and buried. Soft voices murmuring upon the wind drowned it, sweet voices rising above the graves and the monuments, and the folded flags, repeating the litany of the dead. The chant came borne upon the western wind across the bare mountains, and the empty plains, and the rich untilled meadows, and the green uninhabited hills, singing a song that told the pirate sleeper coiled about the yellow bay that all was well with the company of heroes.

A drowsy whisper hovered under the golden haze where the air is honey-sweet and its lips are soft. High deeds, brave words, and the long litany of lovers: Olaf and Ivarr and Niall; and Dunan and Dermot and O'Brien; and Henry and Bruce and Silken Thomas; and Stuart and William and Ormonde; and Fitzgerald and Tone and Sheares; and O'Connell and Pearse and Joyce; and other names of a high company, and snatches of a rebel song.

But while the curving body stirred and murmured and slept again by the edge of the Norsemen's bay, drunk with legends and lulled with rhymes, another sound broke through the soft poetic haze. It gathered up the names of the old towns by the storied rivers and the green meadows and the purple mountains, and flung them like stones upon the tarnished mirror of the waters. It was a harsh sound; a high sound; a sound that echoed and re-echoed among the haunted hills like the scream of the departing swifts. Roscommon, it blared, and Mullingar and Athlone and Ballinasloe and Galway and Limerick and Westport and Cork and Waterford and Tralee. It was the sound of the new poetry; and it was not honey-sweet, and its lips were not soft.

Mr Quill heard it as he stood on the front at Dun Laoghaire looking down at the mail-boat pier. He was not aware of the golden magic that drifted in the silken air about his head; he did not recollect the heroic legends that hung about the bay at which he so short-sightedly gazed; nor did he call to mind the poems he had learned as a boy that celebrated the soft smiling land behind him. He did not know of the wing-eyed Vikings, and the golden coins of Sigtryggr. He did not think of purple tunics and silver belts, and the dim dark echo of battles won in the morning of the world.

He stood dumb with misery, and dazed by the blare of the loudspeakers on the landing-stage announcing the arrival and departure of trains from the four corners of Ireland. He had got into the habit during the past week,

since Caroline went to England, of walking down to watch
the mail-boat sail. He stood alone among the little knot of
watchers that gathered every evening around the Obelisk of
King George IV to see the emigrants embark. They came
in their thousands from the trains, from cars, buses, and on
foot. They came from the dead cliffs, and the blue mountains, and the rich meadows, and the green hills. If they
sang a lament it was because some of them were drunk; for
they too were unaware of the company of heroes that
hovered in the air about their heads. They had their tickets
in their fists and their time was short. They carried bulging cardboard cases, and brown paper parcels, and chick-
ens and eggs and butter wrapped in newspaper. Some of
them slipped their clumsy fingers under their shirts and
blouses and touched the holy medals and the brown
scapulars that they wore about their necks. They wore
rough tweed caps, and shiny serge suits and yellow boots;
they wore cheap red coats, and worn headscarves about
their tangled hair, and walked on crooked high heels below
thick country ankles. Their voices mingled with the blare
of the loudspeakers: thick lilting voices from the south,
soft slurring voices from the west, flat droning voices from
the midlands, hard trenchant voices from the north. They
crowded elbow to elbow at the entrance to the pier, and
swarmed over the boat like flies in Mr Quill's vision. They
kissed and swore and jostled upon the gangways. They
drank whiskey in the saloon bar, and uncorked bottles of
stout in the steerage. They made water in all the lavatories
of the boat, and farted and belched and scratched and
vomited and yawned through rotten teeth; and the air
about them was not honey-sweet and its lips were not soft.
They wept; they roared; they laughed. They sat hunched
on benches, large of foot and heavy of heart, staring out to
sea. They threw orange-peel into the tarnished waters of
the bay. They drank tea out of flasks, and water out of
cardboard cups. They suckled babies with milk out of
bottles, and fed them with sweets out of sticky paper bags.

They curled up on sofas and shut their eyes and tried to sleep. They leaned across the rails and waved to friends and relations. They looked up at the golden haze of the sky and cursed. They thought of little white houses in the flat meadows by the inland rivers. They thought of tiny patches of green imprisoned behind low stone walls on the slopes of blue mountains. They thought of the dead cliffs and the cold Atlantic already flecked with winter foam. They ate thick jam sandwiches and remembered addresses in Manchester, Liverpool and Huddersfield.

And then for an instant they were silent, all of them, as the boat shivered and slid out over the yellow waters, away from the haunted hills and the company of heroes dead and gone. A split second of hopeful silence. But the coiling figure round the bay did not waken even when the loud-speakers blared again, and the voices of the exiles called out again over the slumbering waters as they crowded the decks for one last sight of the smiling land, and the little knot of watchers on the pier.

Smaller and smaller the figures grew, and paler the hills; and the loudspeakers went dead, and the ship slipped over the horizon. The watcher; the friends, the lovers, the fathers and mothers broke up and went away.

Mr Quill was the last to leave. He walked slowly along the front, and sat down on one of the seats. He took out the bank draft for three hundred pounds which had reached him the day before. He looked at it for a long time before putting it back into his wallet again. There were so many things that had to be taken into consideration before he could make up his mind what to do with it. His first impulse had been to send it back to Philip. But then he thought of Caroline. She might fall sick; she might have an accident; she might be out of a job for a long while when her time came. He delayed his decision, allowing the time to pass, refusing to think about it. Mr Quill now knew that everything in life had to be paid for; and that most of it had to be paid in hard cash.

He got up and walked over to the railings above the sea. Shadows were falling across the bay, over the floating orange-skins, and the scraps of paper, and the submerged sewage of a thousand souls. Above, the sky was now a beaten bronze, a shield for the city. And the air was honey-sweet. But Mr Quill was aware of none of this. For him, as for the other watchers, and the teeming crowds on the boat, the romantic experiment was over. The four green fields were in the hands of the receiver.

John Broderick
The Fugitives 70p

With her brother Paddy on the run after an IRA murder,
Lily offers his only safety. In their small Irish home town,
watched constantly by their neighbours – themselves only
evident from the twitching of curtains – the brother and
sister wait.

With the arrival of the sinister Hugh Ward – come to look
after Paddy. Lily knows the overpowering combination
of fear and love as the tension and tragedy looms . . .

'Mr Broderick generates a macabre and even slightly
Gothic atmosphere . . . In his account of sombre and
violent emotions seething beneath a surface of Catholic
pietism – very faithfully rendered – and small town
conventions, he recalls Mauriac' SPECTATOR

The Pilgrimage 50p

Julia needs men in the same way she needs air to breathe . . .
but neither her middle-aged and crippled husband Michael,
nor her lover, Jim, can satisfy her desires. When she
turns to Stephen, Michael's manservant, the under-
currents of tension and emotion between the four run
dangerously strong . . . until, on a pilgrimage to Lourdes,
they reach a startlingly dramatic conclusion . . .

'the most accurately observed Irish novel I have read
in years' BELFAST TELEGRAPH

A Pride of Summer 75p

After twenty years of marriage to the prosperous
Catholic. Tony O'Reilly. Olive leaves home. Deserting
her family she moves in with two protestant old maids.
Rumours start to spread, feeding the sexual tensions
and the old religious and political hatreds. Shaun Lucey,
the whiskey-stained publican, is just one man with a reason
to get back at the old spinsters.

'A witch's cauldron of seething passions' IRISH TIMES

John Broderick
An Apology for Roses 35p

Lust, love, religion and greed . . .

In a small Irish village, Marie Fogarty is very much alive,
very much aware of her need for men. Whether with priest
or commercial traveller, on the seats of a red mini or in a
bedroom – with the statue of the Blessed Virgin decently
draped – Marie scorns guilt and gossip for the warm odours
of the flesh. But to marry, she must fight her mother tooth-
and-nail for the money that can buy respectability.

Christy Brown
Down all the Days 70p

A distillation of Dublin in the tradition of *Ulysses* – its
raging men and lusty women – its drunken furies and its
bawdy laughter – its brutal matings and its frenzied wakes
are captured here in the greatest novel of a generation.

Wild Grow the Lilies 90p

'Will probably be every bit as successful as *Down All The
Days* . . . Never before has so much alcohol been consumed
between book covers! TIMES LITERARY SUPPLEMENT
'Hilarious and randy!' THE TIMES